Going Places

Leonard Michaels

N E W   Y O R K

Going Places

Farrar, Straus & Giroux

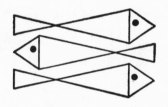

FOR PRISCILLA

CONTENTS

Manikin

At the university she met a Turk who studied physics and spoke foreigner's English which in every turn expressed the unnatural desire to seize idiom and make it speak just for himself. He worked nights as a waiter, summers on construction gangs, and shot pool and played bridge with fraternity boys in order to make small change, and did whatever else he could to protect and supplement his university scholarship, living a mile from campus in a room without sink or closet or decent heating and stealing most of the food he ate, and when the University Hotel was robbed it was the Turk who had done it, an act of such speed the night porter couldn't say when it happened or who rushed in from the street to bludgeon him so murderously he took it in a personal way. On weekends the Turk tutored mediocrities in mathematics and French. . . .

He picked her up at her dormitory, took her to a movie, and later, in his borrowed Chevrolet, drove her into the countryside and with heavy, crocodilean sentences communicated his agony amid the alien corn. She attended with quick, encouraging little nods and stared as if each word crept past her eyes and she felt power gathering in their difficult motion as he leaned toward her and with lips still laboring words made indelible sense, raping her, forcing her to variations of what she never heard of though she was a great reader of avant-garde novels and philosophical commentaries on the modern predicament. . . .

In the cracking, desiccated leather of the Chevrolet she was susceptible to a distinction between life and sensibility, and dropped, like Leda by the swan, squirming, arching, so as not to be touched again, inadvertently, as he poked behind the cushions for the ignition key. She discovered it pulling up her pants and, because it required intelligent speech inconsistent with her moaning, couldn't bring it to his attention; nor would she squat, winding about in her privates, though she hated to see him waste time bunched up twisting wires under the dashboard.

Despite her wild compulsion to talk and despite the frightened, ravenous curiosity of her dormitory clique whom she awakened by sobbing over their beds, Melanie wasn't able to say clearly what finished happening half an hour ago. She remembered the Turk suddenly abandoned English and raved at her in furious Turkish, and she told them about that and about the obscene tattoo flashing on his chest when she ripped his shirt open, and that he stopped the car on a country road and there was a tall hedge, maples, sycamores, and a railroad track nearby, and a train was passing, passing, and passing, and beyond it, her moans, and later an animal trotting quickly on the gravel, and then, with no discontinuity, the motor starting its cough and retch and a cigarette waving at her mouth already lighted as if the worst were over and someone had started thinking of her in another way.

The lights of the university town appeared and she smoked the cigarette as the car went down among them through empty streets, through the residential area of the ethical, economic community and twisted into the main street passing store after store. She saw an armless, naked manikin and felt like that, or like a thalidomide baby, all torso and short-circuited, and then they were into the streets around campus, narrow and shaky with trees, and neither of them said a word as he shifted gears, speeding and slowing and working the car through a passage irregular and yet steady, and enclosed within a greater passage as tangible as the internal arcs of their skulls. At the dormitory he stopped the car. She got out running.

Quigley, Berkowitz and Sax could tell that Melanie Green had been assaulted with insane and exotic cruelty: there were fingerprints on her cheeks the color of tea stains and her stockings hung about her ankles like Hamlet's when he exposed himself to Ophelia and called her a whore. So they sucked cigarettes and urged her to phone the Dean of Women, the police and the immigration authorities, as if disseminating the story among representatives of order would qualify it toward annihilation or render it accessible to a punitive response consistent with national foreign policy. Though none of them saw positive value in Melanie's experience it was true, nevertheless, in no future conversation would she complain about being nineteen and not yet discovered by the right man, as it happened, to rape with. Given her face and legs, *that* had always seemed sick, irritating crap, and in the pits of their minds where there were neither words nor ideas but only raging morality, they took the Turk as poetic justice, fatal male, and measure for measure. Especially since he lived now in those pits vis-à-vis Melanie's father, a bearded rabbi with tear bags. "What if your father knew?" asked Quigley, making a gesture of anxious speculation, slender hands turned out flat, palms up, like a Balinese dancer. Melanie felt annoyed, but at least Quigley was there, sticking out her hands, and could be relied on always to be symbolic of whatever she imagined the situation required.

She didn't tell the rabbi, the Dean of Women, police, or immigration authorities, and didn't tell Harry Stone, her fiancé, with whom she had never had all-the-way sexual intercourse because he feared it might destroy the rhythm of his graduate work in Classics. But once, during Christmas vacation, she flew East to visit him and while standing on a stairway in Cambridge, after dinner and cognac, he let her masturbate him and then lay in bed beside her, brooding, saying little except, "I feel like Seymour," and she answering, "I'm sorry." Quigley, Berkowitz and Sax called him "Harry the fairy," but never in the presence of Melanie who read them his letters, brilliantly exquisite and full of ruthless wit directed at everything, and the girls screamed and could hardly wait till he got his degree and laid her. "It'll be made of porcelain," said Sax, and Melanie couldn't refute the proposition (though the girls always told her everything they did with their boyfriends and she owed them the masturbation story) because they were too hot for physiology and wouldn't listen to the whole story, wouldn't hear its tone or any of its music. They were critical, sophisticated girls and didn't dig mood, didn't savor things. They were too fast, too eager to get the point.

She didn't tell the rabbi or any other authority about the rape, and wouldn't dream of telling Harry Stone because he tended to become irrationally jealous and like homosexual Othello would assume she had gone out with armies of men aside from the Turk, which wasn't true. The Turk had been a casual decision, the only one of its kind, determined by boredom with classes and dateless weekends, and partly by a long-distance phone call to Harry Stone in the middle of the night when she needed his voice and he expressed irritation at having been disturbed while translating a difficult passage of Thucydides for a footnote in his dissertation. Furthermore the Turk was interesting-looking, black eyes, a perfect white bite of teeth between a biggish nose and a cleft chin, and because he was pathetic in his tortuous English going out with him seemed merely an act of charity indifferently performed and it was confirmed as such when he arrived in the old Chevrolet and suggested a cowboy movie. He held the door open for her which she could never expect Harry to do, and he tried to talk to her. To her, she felt—though it was clear that his effort to talk depended very much on her effort to listen.

She went to parties on the two weekends following the rape and sat in darkened rooms while a hashish pipe went around and said things too deep for syntax and giggled hysterically, and in the intimate delirium of faces and darkness asked how one might get in touch with an abortionist if, per chance, one needed one. She didn't talk about the rape but remembered the Turk had held her chin and she felt guilty but resistless and saw that his eyes didn't focus and that, more than anything, lingered in her nerves, like birds screaming and inconsummate. She asked her clique about the signs of pregnancy, then asked herself if she weren't peeing more than usual. It seemed to spear down very hot and hard and longer than before, but she ascribed it to sphincters loosened upon the violent dissolution of the veil between vaginal post and lintel. When she asked the girls about an abortionist they laughed maniacally at the idea that any of them might know such a person, but, one at a time, appeared in her room to whisper names and telephone numbers and tell her about the different techniques and the anesthetic she might expect if the man were considerate or brave enough to give her one. "They're afraid of the cops," said Sax, a tough number from Chicago who had been knocked up twice in her freshman year. "They want you out of the office as soon as possible."

Harry surprised her by coming to town during his intersession break and she was so glad to see him she trembled. She introduced him to her house mother and her clique and he ate dinner with her in the dormitory the first night. The next day he went to classes with her and that evening they ate in the best restaurant in town, which wasn't nearly as good as some Harry knew in the East but it was pretty good, and then they walked in the Midwestern twilight, watching swallows, listening to night hawks whistle, and she felt an accumulation of sympathy in the minutes and the hours which became an urge, a possibility, and then a strong need to tell him, but she chatted mainly about her clique and said, "Quigley has funny nipples and Berkowitz would have a wonderful figure except for her thighs which have no character. I love Sax's figure. It's like a skinny boy's." Harry made an indifferent face and shrugged in his tweeds, but quick frowns twitched after the facts and she went on, encouraged thus, going on, to go on and on. In his hotel room they had necking and writhing, then lay together breathless, tight, indeterminate, until he began talking about his dissertation. "A revo-

lution in scholarship. The vitiation of many tradi-
tional assumptions. They say I write uncommonly
well." She told him about the rape. He sat up with
words about the impossibility of confidence, the be-
trayal of expectations, the end of things. He was
amazed, he said, the world didn't break and the sky
fall down. As far as he was concerned the ceremony
of innocence was drowned. While he packed she
rubbed her knees and stared at him. He noticed her
staring and said, "I don't like you."

Wanda Chung was always in flight around corners, down hallways, up stairs, into bathrooms, and
never spoke to people unless obliged to do so and
then with fleeting, terrified smiles and her eyes
somewhere else. She appeared at no teas or dances,
received no calls and no boys at the reception desk,
and Melanie and her clique gradually came to think
of her as the most interesting girl in the dormitory.
One afternoon after classes they decided to go to her
room and introduce themselves. She wasn't in so
they entered the room and while waiting for her cas-
ually examined her closet which was packed with
dresses and coats carrying the labels of good stores in
San Francisco. Under her bed there were boxes of
new blouses and sweaters, and they discovered her

desk drawers were crammed with candy and empty candy wrappers. They left her room, never returned, and never again made any effort to introduce themselves to her, but Wanda, who for months had harbored a secret yearning to meet Melanie, decided, the day after Harry Stone left town, to go to Melanie's room and present herself: "I am Wanda Chung. I live downstairs. I found this fountain pen. Could it be yours?" She bought a fountain pen and went to Melanie's room and an instant after she knocked at the door she forgot her little speech and her desire to meet Melanie. The door gave way at the vague touch of her knuckles and started opening as if Wanda herself had taken the knob and turned it with the intention of getting into the room and stealing something, which is how she saw it, standing there as the door unbelievably, remorselessly, opened, sucking all motion and feeling out of her limbs and making her more and more thief in the possible eyes of anyone coming along. And then, into her dumb rigidity, swayed naked feet like bell clappers. She saw Melanie Green hanging by the neck, her pelvis twitching. Wanda dashed to the stairs, down to her room, and locked herself inside. She ate candy until she puked in her lap and fell asleep. . . .

When the Turk read about the suicide he said in a slow, sick voice, "She loved me." He got drunk and stumbled through the streets looking for a fight, but bumping strangers and firing clams of spit at their feet wasn't sufficiently provocative, given his de-bauched and fiercely miserable appearance, to get himself punched or cursed or even shoved a little. He ended the night in a scrubby field tearing at an oak tree with his fingernails, rolling in its roots, hammer-ing grass, cursing the sources of things until, in a shy, gentle way, Melanie drifted up out of the dew. He refused to acknowledge her presence but then couldn't tolerate being looked at in silence and yelled at her in furious Turkish. She came closer. He seized her in his arms and they rolled together in the grass until he found himself screaming through his teeth because, however much of himself he lavished on her, she was dead.

City Boy

"**P**HILLIP," SHE SAID, "THIS IS CRAZY."

I didn't agree or disagree. She wanted some answer. I bit her neck. She kissed my ear. It was nearly three in the morning. We had just returned. The apartment was dark and quiet. We were on the living-room floor and she repeated, "Phillip, this is crazy." Her crinoline broke under us like cinders. Furniture loomed all around—settee, chairs, a table with a lamp. Pictures were cloudy blotches drifting above. But no lights, no things to look at, no eyes in her head. She was underneath me and warm. The rug was warm, soft as mud, deep. Her crinoline cracked like sticks. Our naked bellies clapped together. Air fired out like farts. I took it as applause. The chandelier clicked. The clock ticked as if to split its glass.

"Phillip," she said, "this is crazy." A little voice against the grain and power. Not enough to stop me. Yet once I had been a man of feeling. We went to concerts, walked in the park, trembled in the maid's room. Now in the foyer, a flash of hair and claws. We stumbled to the living-room floor. She said, "Phillip, this is crazy." Then silence, except in my head where a conference table was set up, ashtrays scattered about. Priests, ministers and rabbis were rushing to take seats. I wanted their opinion, but came. They vanished. A voice lingered, faintly crying, "You could mess up the rug, Phillip, break something . . ." Her fingers pinched my back like ants. I expected a remark to kill good death. She said nothing. The breath in her nostrils whipped mucus. It cracked in my ears like flags. I dreamed we were in her mother's Cadillac, trailing flags. I heard her voice before I heard the words. "Phillip, this is crazy. My parents are in the next room." Her cheek jerked against mine, her breasts were knuckles in my nipples. I burned. Good death was killed. I burned with hate. A rabbi shook his finger, "You shouldn't hate." I lifted on my elbows, sneering in pain. She wrenched her hips, tightened muscles in belly and neck. She said, "Move." It was imperative to move. Her parents were thirty feet away. Down the hall between Utrillos and Vlamincks, through the door, flick the light and I'd see them. Maybe like us, Mr. Cohen adrift on the missus. Hair sifted down my cheek. "Let's go to the maid's room," she whispered. I was reassured. She tried to move. I kissed her mouth. Her crinoline smashed like sugar. Pig that I was, I couldn't move. The clock ticked hysterically. Ticks piled up like insects. Muscles lapsed in her thighs. Her fingers scratched on my neck as if looking for buttons. She slept. I sprawled like a bludgeoned pig, eyes open, loose lips. I flopped into sleep, in her, in the rug, in our scattered clothes.

Dawn hadn't shown between the slats in the blinds. Her breathing sissed in my ear. I wanted to sleep more, but needed a cigarette. I thought of the cold avenue, the lonely subway ride. Where could I buy a newspaper, a cup of coffee? This was crazy, dangerous, a waste of time. The maid might arrive, her parents might wake. I had to get started. My hand pushed along the rug to find my shirt, touched a brass lion's paw, then a lamp cord.

A naked heel bumped wood.

She woke, her nails in my neck. "Phillip, did you hear?" I whispered, "Quiet." My eyes rolled like Milton's. Furniture loomed, whirled. "Dear God," I prayed, "save my ass." The steps ceased. Neither of us breathed. The clock ticked. She trembled. I pressed my cheek against her mouth to keep her from talking. We heard pajamas rustle, phlegmy breathing, fingernails scratching hair. A voice, "Veronica, don't you think it's time you sent Phillip home?"

A murmur of assent started in her throat, swept to my cheek, fell back drowned like a child in a well. Mr. Cohen had spoken. He stood ten inches from our legs. Maybe less. It was impossible to tell. His fingernails grated through hair. His voice hung in the dark with the quintessential question. Mr. Cohen, scratching his crotch, stood now as never in the light. Considerable. No tool of his wife, whose energy in business kept him eating, sleeping, overlooking the park. Pinochle change in his pocket four nights a week. But were they his words? Or was he the oracle of Mrs. Cohen, lying sleepless, irritated, waiting for him to get me out? I didn't breathe. I didn't move. If he had come on his own he would leave without an answer. His eyes weren't adjusted to the dark. He couldn't see. We lay at his feet like worms. He scratched, made smacking noises with his mouth.

The question of authority is always with us. Who is responsible for the triggers pulled, buttons pressed, the gas, the fire? Doubt banged my brain.

My heart lay in the fist of intellect, which squeezed out feeling like piss out of kidneys. Mrs. Cohen's voice demolished doubt, feeling, intellect. It ripped from the bedroom.

"For God's sake, Morris, don't be banal. Tell the schmuck to go home and keep his own parents awake all night, if he has any."

Veronica's tears slipped down my cheeks. Mr. Cohen sighed, shuffled, made a strong voice. "Veronica, tell Phillip . . ." His foot came down on my ass. He drove me into his daughter. I drove her into his rug.

"I don't believe it," he said.

He walked like an antelope, lifting hoof from knee, but stepped down hard. Sensitive to the danger of movement, yet finally impulsive, flinging his pot at the earth in order to cross it. His foot brought me his weight and character, a hundred fifty-five pounds of stomping shlemiel, in a mode of apprehension so primal we must share it with bugs. Let armies stomp me to insensate pulp—I'll yell "Cohen" when he arrives.

Veronica squealed, had a contraction, fluttered, gagged a shriek, squeezed, and up like a frog out of the hand of a child I stood spread-legged, bolt naked, great with eyes. Mr. Cohen's face was eyes in my eyes. A secret sharer. We faced each other like men accidentally met in hell. He retreated flapping, moaning, "I will not believe it one bit."

Veronica said, "Daddy?"

"Who else you no good bum?"

The rug raced. I smacked against blinds, glass broke and I whirled. Veronica said, "Phillip," and I went off in streaks, a sparrow in the room, here, there, early American, baroque and rococo. Veronica wailed, "Phillip." Mr. Cohen screamed, "I'll kill him." I stopped at the door, seized the knob. Mrs. Cohen yelled from the bedroom, "Morris, did something break? Answer me."

"I'll kill that bastid."

"Morris, if something broke you'll rot for a month."

"Mother, stop it," said Veronica. "Phillip, come back."

The door slammed. I was outside, naked as a wolf.

I needed poise. Without poise the street was impossible. Blood shot to my brain, thought blossomed. I'd walk on my hands. Beards were fashionable. I kicked up my feet, kicked the elevator button, faced the door and waited. I bent one elbow like a knee. The posture of a clothes model, easy, poised. Blood coiled down to my brain, weeds bourgeoned. I had

made a bad impression. There was no other way to
see it. But all right. We needed a new beginning.
Everyone does. Yet how few of us know when it arrives. Mr. Cohen had never spoken to me before; this
was a breakthrough. There had been a false element
in our relationship. It was wiped out. I wouldn't kid
myself with the idea that he had nothing to say. I'd
had enough of his silent treatment. It was worth being naked to see how mercilessly I could think. I had
his number. Mrs. Cohen's, too. I was learning every
second. I was a city boy. No innocent shitkicker from
Jersey. I was the A train, the Fifth Avenue bus. I
could be a cop. My name was Phillip, my style New
York City. I poked the elevator button with my toe. It
rang in the lobby, waking Ludwig. He'd come for me,
rotten with sleep. Not the first time. He always took
me down, walked me through the lobby and let me
out on the avenue. Wires began tugging him up the
shaft. I moved back, conscious of my genitals hanging upside down. Absurd consideration; we were
both men one way or another. There were social dis-
tinctions enforced by his uniform, but they would
vanish at the sight of me. "The unaccommodated
thing itself." "Off ye lendings!" The greatest play is
about a naked man. A picture of Lear came to me,
naked, racing through the wheat. I could be cool. I
thought of Ludwig's uniform, hat, whipcord collar. It

signified his authority. Perhaps he would be annoyed, in his authority, by the sight of me naked.
Few people woke him at such hours. Worse, I never
tipped him. Could I have been so indifferent month
after month? In a crisis you discover everything.
Then it's too late. Know yourself, indeed. You need a
crisis every day. I refused to think about it. I sent my
mind after objects. It returned with the chairs, settee, table and chandelier. Where were my clothes? I
sent it along the rug. It found buttons, eagles
stamped in brass. I recognized them as the buttons
on Ludwig's coat. Eagles, beaks like knives, shrieking
for tips. Fuck'm, I thought. Who's Ludwig? A big
coat, a whistle, white gloves and a General MacAr-
thur hat. I could understand him completely. He
couldn't begin to understand me. A naked man is
mysterious. But aside from that, what did he know? I
dated Veronica Cohen and went home late. Did he
know I was out of work? That I lived in a slum downtown? Of course not.

Possibly under his hat was a filthy mind. He imagined Veronica and I might be having sexual intercourse. He resented it. Not that he hoped for the priv-
ilege himself, in his coat and soldier hat, but he had
a proprietary interest in the building and its residents. I came from another world. *The* other world
against which Ludwig defended the residents.

Wasn't I like a burglar sneaking out late, making him my accomplice? I undermined his authority, his dedication. He despised me. It was obvious. But no one thinks such thoughts. It made me laugh to think them. My genitals jumped. The elevator door slid open. He didn't say a word. I padded inside like a seal. The door slid shut. Instantly, I was ashamed of myself, thinking as I had about him. I had no right. A better man than I. His profile was an etching by Dürer. Good peasant stock. How had he fallen to such work? Existence precedes essence. At the controls, silent, enduring, he gave me strength for the street. Perhaps the sun would be up, birds in the air. The door slid open. Ludwig walked ahead of me through the lobby. He needed new heels. The door of the lobby was half a ton of glass, encased in iron vines and leaves. Not too much for Ludwig. He turned, looked down into my eyes. I watched his lips move.

"I vun say sumding. Yur bisniss vot you do. Bud vy you mek her miserable? Nod led her slip. She has beks unter her eyes."

Ludwig had feelings. They spoke to mine. Beneath the uniform, a man. Essence precedes existence. Even rotten with sleep, thick, dry bags under his eyes, he saw, he sympathized. The discretion demanded by his job forbade anything tangible, a sweater, a hat. "Ludwig," I whispered, "you're all right." It didn't matter if he heard me. He knew I said something. He knew it was something nice. He grinned, tugged the door open with both hands. I slapped out onto the avenue. I saw no one, dropped to my feet and glanced back through the door. Perhaps for the last time. I lingered, indulged a little melancholy. Ludwig walked to a couch in the rear of the lobby. He took off his coat, rolled it into a pillow and lay down. I had never stayed to see him do that before, but always rushed off to the subway. As if I were indifferent to the life of the building. Indeed, like a burglar. I seized the valuables and fled to the subway. I stayed another moment, watching good Ludwig, so I could hate myself. He assumed the modest, saintly posture of sleep. One leg here, the other there. His good head on his coat. A big arm across his stomach, the hand between his hips. He made a fist and punched up and down.

I went down the avenue, staying close to the buildings. Later I would work up a philosophy. Now I wanted to sleep, forget. I hadn't the energy for moral complexities: Ludwig cross-eyed, thumping his pelvis in such a nice lobby. Mirrors, glazed pots, rubber plants ten feet high. As if he were generating all of it. As if it were part of his job. I hurried. The buildings were on my left, the park on my right. There were doormen in all the buildings; God knows what was in the park. No cars were moving. No people in sight. Streetlights glowed in a receding sweep down to Fifty-ninth Street and beyond. A wind pressed my face like Mr. Cohen's breath. Such hatred. Imponderable under any circumstances, a father cursing his daughter. Why? A fright in the dark? Freud said things about fathers and daughters. It was too obvious, too hideous. I shuddered and went more quickly. I began to run. In a few minutes I was at the spit-mottled steps of the subway. I had hoped for vomit. Spit is no challenge for bare feet. Still, I wouldn't complain. It was sufficiently disgusting to make me live in spirit. I went down the steps flatfooted, stamping, elevated by each declension. I was a city boy, no mincing creep from the sticks.

A Negro man sat in the change booth. He wore glasses, a white shirt, black knit tie and a silver tie clip. I saw a mole on his right cheek. His hair had spots of grey, as if strewn with ashes. He was reading a newspaper. He didn't hear me approach, didn't see my eyes take him in, figure him out. Shirt, glasses, tie—I knew how to address him. I coughed. He looked up.

"Sir, I don't have any money. Please let me through the turnstile. I come this way every week and will certainly pay you the next time."

[2 7]

He merely looked at me. Then his eyes flashed like fangs. Instinctively, I guessed what he felt. He didn't owe favors to a white man. He didn't have to bring his allegiance to the Transit Authority into question for my sake.

"Hey, man, you naked?"

"Yes."

"Step back a little."

I stepped back.

"You're naked."

I nodded.

"Get your naked ass the hell out of here."

"Sir," I said, "I know these are difficult times, but can't we be reasonable? I know that . . ."

"Scat, mother, go home."

I crouched as if to dash through the turnstile. He crouched, too. It proved he would come after me. I shrugged, turned back toward the steps. The city was infinite. There were many other subways. But why had he become so angry? Did he think I was a bigot? Maybe I was running around naked to get him upset. His anger was incomprehensible otherwise. It made me feel like a bigot. First a burglar, then a bigot. I needed a cigarette. I could hardly breathe. Air was too good for me. At the top of the steps, staring down, stood Veronica. She had my clothes.

"Poor, poor," she said.

I said nothing. I snatched my underpants and put them on. She had my cigarettes ready. I tried to light one, but the match failed. I threw down the cigarette and the matchbook. She retrieved them as I dressed. She lit the cigarette for me and held my elbow to help me keep my balance. I finished dressing, took the cigarette. We walked back toward her building. The words "thank you" sat in my brain like driven spikes. She nibbled her lip.

"How are things at home?" My voice was casual and morose, as if no answer could matter.

"All right," she said, her voice the same as mine. She took her tone from me. I liked that sometimes, sometimes not. Now I didn't like it. I discovered I was angry. Until she said that, I had no idea I was angry. I flicked the cigarette into the gutter and suddenly I knew why. I didn't love her. The cigarette sizzled in the gutter. Like truth. I didn't love her. Black hair, green eyes, I didn't love her. Slender legs. I didn't. Last night I had looked at her and said to myself, "I hate communism." Now I wanted to step on her head. Nothing less than that would do. If it was a perverted thought, then it was a perverted thought. I wasn't afraid to admit it to myself.

"All right? Really? Is that true?"

Blah, blah, blah. Who asked those questions? A zombie; not Phillip of the foyer and rug. He died in flight. I was sorry, sincerely sorry, but with clothes on my back I knew certain feelings would not survive humiliation. It was so clear it was thrilling. Perhaps she felt it, too. In any case she would have to accept it. The nature of the times. We are historical creatures. Veronica and I were finished. Before we reached her door I would say deadly words. They'd come in a natural way, kill her a little. Veronica, let me step on your head or we're through. Maybe we're through, anyway. It would deepen her looks, give philosophy to what was only charming in her face. The dawn was here. A new day. Cruel, but change is cruel. I could bear it. Love is infinite and one. Women are not. Neither are men. The human condition. Nearly unbearable.

"No, it's not true," she said.

"What's not?"

"Things aren't all right at home."

I nodded intelligently, sighed, "Of course not. Tell me the truth, please. I don't want to hear anything else."

"Daddy had a heart attack."

"Oh God," I yelled. "Oh God, no."

I seized her hand, dropped it. She let it fall. I

seized it again. No use. I let it fall. She let it drift between us. We stared at one another. She said, "What were you going to say? I can tell you were going to say something."

I stared, said nothing.

"Don't feel guilty, Phillip. Let's just go back to the apartment and have some coffee."

"What can I say?"

"Don't say anything. He's in the hospital and my mother is there. Let's just go upstairs and not say anything."

"Not say anything. Like moral imbeciles go slurp coffee and not say anything? What are we, nihilists or something? Assassins? Monsters?"

"Phillip, there's no one in the apartment. I'll make us coffee and eggs . . ."

"How about a roast beef? Got a roast beef in the freezer?"

"Phillip, he's *my* father."

We were at the door. I rattled. I was in a trance. This was life. Death!

"Indeed, your father. I'll accept that. I can do no less."

"Phillip, shut up. Ludwig."

The door opened. I nodded to Ludwig. What did he know about life and death? Give him a uniform and a quiet lobby—that's life and death. In the elevator he took the controls. "Always got a hand on the controls, eh Ludwig?"

Veronica smiled in a feeble, grateful way. She liked to see me get along with the help. Ludwig said, "Dots right."

"Ludwig has been our doorman for years, Phillip. Ever since I was a little girl."

"Wow," I said.

"Dots right."

The door slid open. Veronica said, "Thank you, Ludwig." I said, "Thank you, Ludwig."

"Vulcum."

"Vulcum? You mean, 'welcome'? Hey, Ludwig, how long you been in this country?"

Veronica was driving her key into the door.

"How come you never learned to talk American, baby?"

"Phillip, come here."

"I'm saying something to Ludwig."

"Come here right now."

"I have to go, Ludwig."

"Vulcum."

She went directly to the bathroom. I waited in the hallway between Vlamincks and Utrillos. The Utrillos were pale and flat. The Vlamincks were thick, twisted and red. Raw meat on one wall, dry stone on the other. Mrs. Cohen had an eye for contrasts. I heard Veronica sob. She ran water in the sink, sobbed, sat down, peed. She saw me looking and kicked the door shut.

"At a time like this . . ."

"I don't like you looking."

"Then why did you leave the door open? You obviously don't know your own mind."

"Go away, Phillip. Wait in the living room."

"Just tell me why you left the door open."

"Phillip, you're going to drive me nuts. Go away. I can't do a damn thing if I know you're standing there."

The living room made me feel better. The settee, the chandelier full of teeth and the rug were company. Mr. Cohen was everywhere, a simple, diffuse presence. He jingled change in his pocket, looked out the window and was happy he could see the park. He took a little antelope step and tears came into my eyes. I sat among his mourners. A rabbi droned platitudes: Mr. Cohen was generous, kind, beloved by his wife and daughter. "How much did he weigh?" I shouted. The phone rang.

Veronica came running down the hall. I went and stood at her side when she picked up the phone. I stood dumb, stiff as a hatrack. She was whimpering, "Yes, yes . . ." I nodded my head yes, yes, thinking it was better than no, no. She put the phone down.

"It was my mother. Daddy's all right. Mother is staying with him in his room at the hospital and they'll come home together tomorrow."

Her eyes looked at mine. At them as if they were as flat and opaque as hers. I said in a slow, stupid voice, "You're allowed to do that? Stay overnight in a hospital with a patient? Sleep in his room?" She continued looking at my eyes. I shrugged, looked down. She took my shirt front in a fist like a bite. She whispered. I said, "What?" She whispered again, "Fuck me." The clock ticked like crickets. The Vlamincks spilled blood. We sank into the rug as if it were quicksand.

Crossbones

At THE END OF THE SUMMER, OR THE YEAR, OR
when he could do more with his talent than play
guitar in a Village strip joint . . . and after con-
sidering his talent for commitment and reluctance
she found reluctance in her own heart and marriage
talk became desultory, specifics dim, ghostly, lost in
bed with Myron doing wrong things, "working on"
her, discovering epileptic dysrhythmia in her hips
and he asked about it and she said it hurt her someplace but not, she insisted, in her head, and they
fought the next morning and the next as if ravenous
for intimacy and disgraced themselves yelling, be-
coming intimate with neighbors, and the superin-
tendent brought them complaints which would have
meant nothing if they hadn't exhausted all desire

for loud, broad strokes, but now, conscious of complaints, they thrust along the vital horizontal with silent, stiletto words, and later in the narrowed range of their imaginations could find no adequate mode of retraction, so wounds festered, burgeoning lurid weeds, poisoning thought, dialogue, and the simple air of their two-room apartment (which had seemed with its view of the Jersey cliffs so much larger than now) now seemed too thick to breathe, or to see through to one another, but they didn't say a word about breaking up, even experimentally, for whatever their doubts about one another, their doubts about other others and the city—themselves adrift in it among messy one-night stands—were too frightening and at least they had, in one another, what they had: Sarah had Myron Bronsky, gloomy brown eyes, a guitar in his hands as mystical and tearing as, say, Lorca, though Myron's particular hands derived from dancing, clapping Hasidim; and he had Sarah Nilsin, Minnesota blonde, long bones, arctic schizophrenia in the gray infinities of her eyes, and a turn for lyric poems derived from piratical saga masters. Rare, but opposites cleave in the divisive angularities of Manhattan and, as the dialectics of embattled individuation became more intense, these two cleaved more tightly: if Sarah, out for groceries, hadn't returned in twenty minutes,

Myron punched a wall, pulverizing the music in his knuckles, but punched, punched until she flung through the door shrieking stop; and he, twenty minutes late from work, found Sarah in kerchief, coat, and gloves, the knotted cloth beneath her chin a little stone proclaiming wild indifference to what the nighttime street could hold, since it held most for him if she were raped and murdered in it. After work he ran home. Buying a quart of milk and a pack of cigarettes, she suffered stomach cramps.

Then a letter came from St. Cloud, Minnesota. Sarah's father was going to visit them next week.

She sewed curtains, squinting down into the night, plucking thread with pricked, exquisite finger-tips. He painted walls lately punched. She bought plants for the windowsills, framed and hung three Japanese prints, and painted the hall toilet opaque, flat yellow. On his knees until sunrise four days in a row, he sanded, then varnished floor boards until the oak bubbled up its blackest grain, turbulent and pet-rified, and Monday dawned on Sarah ironing dresses —more than enough to last her father's visit—and Myron already twice shaved, shining all his shoes, urging her to hurry.

In its mute perfection their apartment now had the air of a well-beaten slave, simultaneously alive and dead, and reflected, like an emanation of their

nerves, a severe, hectic harmony; but it wouldn't
have mattered if the new curtains, pictures, and boiling floors yelled reeking spiritual shambles because
Sarah's father wasn't that kind of minister. His ser-
mons alluded more to Heidegger and Sartre than
Christ, he lifted weights, smoked two packs of cigarettes a day, drove a green Jaguar and, since the
death of Sarah's mother a year ago in a state insane
asylum, had seen species of love in all human rela-
tions. And probably at this very moment, taking the
banked curves of the Pennsylvania Turnpike,
knuckles pale on the walnut wheel, came man and
machine leaning as one toward Jersey, and beyond
that toward love.

Their sense of all this drove them, wrenched
them out of themselves, onto their apartment until
nothing more could make it coincident with what he
would discover in it anyway, and they had now only
their own absolute physical being still to work on, at
nine o'clock, when Myron dashed out to the cleaners
for shirts, trousers and jackets, then dressed in fresh
clothing while Sarah slammed and smeared the iron
down the board as if increasingly sealed in the mo-
mentum of brute work, and then, standing behind
her, lighting a cigarette, Myron was whispering as if
to himself that she must hurry and she was turning
from the board and in the same motion hurled the

iron, lunging after it with nails and teeth before it exploded against the wall and Myron, instantly, hideously understood that the iron, had it struck him, had to burn his flesh and break his bones, flew to meet her with a scream and fists banging her mouth as they locked, winding, fusing to one convulsive beast reeling off walls, tables and chairs, with ashtrays, books, lamps shooting away with pieces of themselves, and he punched out three of her teeth and strangled her until she dissolved in his hands and she scratched his left eye blind—but there was hope in corneal transplantation that he would see through it again—and they were strapped in bandages, twisted and stiff with pain a week after Sarah's father didn't arrive and they helped one another walk slowly up the steps of the municipal building to buy a marriage license.

Sticks and Stones

It was a blind date. She met me at the door and smiled nicely. I could tell she was disappointed. Fortunately, I had brought a bottle of bourbon. An expensive brand, though not a penny too much for a positive *Weltanschauung*. I felt disappointed too. We finished the bourbon and were sitting on the couch. She stuttered the tale of her life and named her favorite authors. I'd never met a girl who stuttered. Our hands became interlocked and hot, our knees touched. Both of us were crying. I cried for her. She, moved by my tears, cried for me. Beyond the room, our sobs, and her breaking, retrogressive voice, I heard church bells. I squeezed her hands, shook my head and staggered from the couch to a window. Glass broke, I fainted, and minutes later awoke on a porch just below the window. She was kneeling beside my head, smoking a cigarette. I heard her voice repeating consonants, going on with the story of her life—a bad man, accident, disease. Broken glass lay about me like stars. Church bells rang the hour, then the half hour. I lay still, thinking nothing, full of mood. Cloth moved smoothly across her thighs as she breathed and rocked to the measures of her story. Despicable as it may seem, that made me sexual. I lifted on an elbow. The sight of my face with the moon shining in it surprised her. She stopped telling her story and said, "No, I d-don't want t-to. . . ." Our eyelids were thick with water. We shook like unhealthy, feverish things.

There was a reason for not having called her again. Shame, disgust, what have you? When I saw her in the street I would run. I saw her there often, and I ran hundreds of miles. My legs became strong, my chest and lungs immense. Soon I could run like a nimble dog. I could wheel abruptly, scramble left or right and go for half the day. I could leap fences and automobiles, run from roof to roof, spring deadly air shafts, and snap in middle flight to gain the yard that saved my life. Once I caught a sparrow smack in my teeth and bit off his head. Spitting feathers and blood, I felt like an eagle. But I was not, and good things, however vigorous, come to an end. At least

for me. I was neither Nietzsche, Don Juan, nor Cha-
teaubriand. My name was Phillip. As I resolved to
stand and started practicing postures, a friend who
knew the girl came and said she wasn't reproachful.
I ought to call her on the phone. It didn't sound true,
but he insisted. She wanted to see me again, at least
as an acquaintance. She would be spared the impli-
cations of my flight. I could rest in body and mind.
Next time I saw her in the street I ran faster than
before, my hair flying, my eyes big. I ran half the day
and all that night.

My friend came again. Running alongside, he
shouted that he had had her too. We stopped.

"Do you mind?" he asked. It had bothered him
so much he couldn't sleep.

"Mind?" I kissed him on the cheek and slapped
his back. Was I happy? The answer is yes. I laughed
till my sight was bleary. My ribs, spreading with
pleasure, made a noise like wheezy old wood. My
friend began laughing, too, and it was a conflation of
waters, lapping and overlapping.

A crooked nose and small, blue eyes—Henry. A
nose, eyes, a curious mouth, a face, my own felt face
behind my eyes, an aspect of my mind, a habit of my
thought—my friend, Henry. The sight of him was

mysterious news, like myself surprised in a mirror, at once strange and familiar. He was tall and went loose and swinging in his stride. Degas dreamed the motion of that dance, a whirl of long bones through streets and rooms. I was shorter, narrower, and conservative in motion. A sharp compliment striding at his side. As Henry was open, I was close, slipping into my parts for endless consultation, like a poker player checking possibilities at the belt. He and I. Me and him. Such opposite adaptations contradict the logic of life, abolish Darwin, testify to miracle and God. I never voiced this idea, but I would think: "Henry, you ought to be dead and utterly vanished, decomposed but for the splinter of tibula or jawbone locked in bog, or part of a boulder, baked, buried, and one with rock." I meant nothing malicious; just the wonder of it.

Now, in company, Henry would grin, expose his dearly familiar chipped front tooth, and whisper, "Tell them how you fell out the window."

"Out the window," people would shout. "You fell out the window? What window?"

I told the story, but declined the honor of being hero. "No, no, not I—this fellow I know—happened to him. Young man out of a job, about my age, depressed about life and himself. You must know the type—can't find meaningful work, spends a lot of time in the movies, wasting . . .

"It was suggested he call a certain girl named Marjorie, herself out of work, not seeing anyone in particular. He asked why out of work. They told him she had had an accident and lived on the insurance payments. Pretty girl? 'Not what you would call pretty. Interesting-looking, bright.' So he called and she said glad to see him, come by, bring something to drink. She had a stutter. It annoyed him, but not so much as her enthusiasm. Anyhow, he was committed. He went with a bottle, and though she was interesting-looking, he was disappointed and began straight in to drink and drink. Perhaps disappointed, too, she drank as fast and as much. The liquor qualified their sense of one another and themselves. Soon they sat on the couch and were full of expectations, drinking, drinking, chatting. He told her about his life, the jobs he had lost, how discontented he felt, and about his one good friend. She followed in a gentle, pleasing way, ooing and clucking. He said there were no frontiers left, nothing for a man to do but explore his own mind and go to the movies. She agreed and said she spent a lot of time just looking in a mirror. Then she came closer and told him about her life. He came closer, too, and fondled her fingertips. She had been raised in an orphanage. He pressed her palms. She had gone to work in a factory. He held her wrists. In an accident at the factory, her leg was bashed and permanently damaged. His hands slid up and down her arms. She limped slightly but the company paid. She didn't mind the limp. He shook his head no. The scars on her face made her look a bit tough; that bothered her. He moaned. She pulled up her dress, showed him the damage, and he began to cry as he snapped it down again. She cried too and pulled it back up. He stumbled from the couch, crying, punching his fists together as he went to the window. Trying to open it he fell through and was nearly killed."

People loved the story and Henry cackled for more.

"You're such a jerk," he said. My heart lunged fiercely with pleasure.

How I carried on. Henry urged me. I carried on and on. Everyone laughed when I fell out the window. No one asked what happened next. Anyhow, the tale of abused and abandoned femininity is pathetic and tediously familiar. Only low, contemptible men who take more pleasure in telling it than doing it would tell it. I stopped for a while after I had a dream in which Henry wanted to kill me.

"Me?" I asked.

"That's right, scum. You!"

Only a dream, but so is life. I took it seriously. Did it warn me of a disaster on the way? Did it indicate a fearful present fact? I studied Henry. Indeed, his face had changed. Never a handsome face, but now, like his face in the dream, it was strangely uncertain, darker, nasty about the edges of the eyes and mouth. Dirty little pimples dotted his neck, and the front chipped tooth gave a new quality to his smile, something asymmetrical, imbecilic and obscene. He looked dissolute and suicidal.

He rarely came to visit me anymore, but we met in the street. Our talk would be more an exchange of looks than words. He looked at me as if I were bleeding. I looked at him quizzically. I looked at him with irony; he returned it with innocence. He burst out laughing. I smiled and looked ready to share the joke. He looked blank, as if I were about to tell him what it was. I grinned, he sneered, he smiled, I frowned, I frowned, he was pained. He looked pained, I looked at my shoes. He looked at my shoes, I looked at his. We looked at one another and he mentioned a mutual friend.

"An idiot," I said.

"A pig."

"Intolerable neurotic."

"Nauseating . . . psychotic."

Then silence. Then he might start, "You know, his face, those weirdly colored eyes . . ."

"Yes," I would say. They were the color of mine. I yawned and scratched at my cheek, though I wasn't sleepy and felt no itch. Our eyes slipped to the corners of the squalid world. Life seemed merely miserable.

Afterwards, alone in my apartment, I had accidents. A glass slipped out of my hand one night, smashed on the floor and cut my shin. When I lifted my pants leg to see the cut, my other leg kicked it. I collapsed on the floor. My legs fought with kicks and scrapes till both lay bleeding, jerky, broken and jointless.

Lose a job, you will find another; break an arm, it soon will heal; ditched by a woman, well

> I don't care if my baby leaves me flat,
> I got forty 'leven others if it come to that.

But a friend! My own felt face. An aspect of my mind. He and I. Me and him. There were no others. I smoked cigarettes and stayed up late staring at a wall. Trying to think, I ran the streets at night. My lungs were thrilled by darkness. Occasionally, I saw Henry and he, too, was running. With so much on our minds, we never stopped to chat, but merely waved and ran on. Now and then we ran side by side for a couple of hundred miles, both of us silent except for the gasping and hissing of our mouths and the cluttered thumping of our feet. He ran as fast as I. Neither of us thought to race, but we might break silence after some wonderful show of the other's speed and call: "Hey, all right." Or, after one of us had executed a brilliant swerve and leap, the other might exclaim, "Bitching good."

Alone, going at high moderate speed one night, I caught a glimpse of Henry walking with a girl. She seemed to limp. I slowed and followed them, keeping well back and low to the ground. They went to a movie theater. I slipped in after they did and took a seat behind theirs. When the girl spoke, I leaned close. She stuttered. It was Marjorie. They kissed. She coiled slow ringlets in the back of his head. I left my seat and paced in the glassy lobby. My heart knocked to get free of my chest and glide up amid the chandeliers. They seemed much in love, childish and animal. He chittered little monkey things to her. There was a coy note in her stutter. They passed without noticing me and stopped under the marquee. Henry lighted a cigarette. She watched as if it were a spectacle for kings. As the fire took life in his eyes, and smoke sifted backward to membranes of his throat, she asked, "What did you think of the m-m-movie, Hen Hen?" His glance became fine, blue as the filament of smoke sliding upward and swaying to breezes no more visible, and vastly less subtle, than the myriad, shifting discriminations that gave sense and value to his answer. "A movie is a complex thing. Images. Actors. I can't quite say." He stared at her without a word. She clucked helplessly. All was light between them. It rose out of warmth. They kissed.

Now I understood and felt much relieved. Henry cared a great deal about movies and he had found someone to whom he could talk about them. Though he hadn't asked me to, I told my story again one evening in company. My voice was soft, but enthusiastic:

"This fellow, ordinary chap with the usual worries about life, had a date to go to the movies with a girl who was quite sweet and pretty and a wonderful conversationalist. She wore a faded gingham blouse, a flowery print skirt and sandals. She limped a bit and had a vague stutter. Her nails were bitten to the neural sheath in finger and toe. She had a faint but regular tic in her left cheek. Throughout the movie she scratched her knees.

"It was a foreign movie about wealthy Italians, mainly a statuesque blonde and a dark, speedy little man who circled about her like a house fly. At last, weary of his constant buzz, she reclined on a bed in his mother's apartment and he did something to her. Afterwards she laughed a great deal, and, near the end of the movie, she discovered an interlocking wire fence. Taking hold with both hands, she clung there while the camera moved away and looked about the city. The movie ended with a study of a street lamp. It had a powerful effect on this fellow and his date. They fell in love before it was half over, and left the theater drunk on the images of the blonde and the speedy little man. He felt the special pertinence of the movie and was speechless. She honored his silence and was speechless, too. Both of them being consciously modern types, they did the thing as soon as they got to her apartment. An act of recognition. A testimony, he thought, to their respect for one another and an agreement to believe their love was more than physical. Any belief needs ritual; so this one. Ergo, the beastly act. Unless it's done, you know, 'a great Prince in prison lies.' Now they could know one another. No longer drunk, they sat disheveled and gloomy on her living-room floor. Neither looked at the other's face, and she, for the sake of motion, scratched her knees. At last, she rose and went to take a shower. When the door shut behind her, he imagined he heard a sob. He crushed his cigarette, went to the window, and flung himself out to the mercy of the night. He has these awful headaches now and constant back pains."

People thought it was a grand story. Henry looked at me till his eyes went click and his mouth resolved into a sneer.

"Ever get a headache in this spot?" He asked, tapping the back of his head.

"Sometimes," I answered, leaning toward him and smiling.

"Then look out. It's a bad sign. It means you've got a slipped disc and probably need an operation. They might have to cut your head off."

Everyone laughed, though no one more than I. Then I got a headache and trembled for an hour. Henry wanted me to have a slipped disc.

Such a man was a threat to the world and public denunciation was in order. I considered beginning work on a small tract about evil, personified by Henry. But I really had nothing to say. He had done me no injury. My dream, however, was obviously the truth: he wanted to kill me. Perhaps, inadvertently, I had said or done something to insult him. A gentleman, says Lord Chesterfield, never unintentionally insults anyone. But I didn't fancy myself a gentleman. Perhaps there was some aspect of my character he thought ghastly. After all, you may know a person for centuries before discovering a hideous peculiarity in him. I considered changing my character, but I didn't know how or what to change. It was perplexing. Henry's character was vile, so I would change mine. I hadn't ever thought his character was vile before. Now, all I had to do was think: "Henry." Vile, oh vile, vile. It would require a revolution in me. Better that than lose a friend. No; better to be yourself and proud. Tell Henry to go to hell. But a real friend goes to hell himself. One afternoon, on my way to hell, I turned a corner and was face to face with Marjorie. She stopped and smiled. Behind her I could see flames. Fluttering down the wind came the sound of prayer.

There was no reason to run. I stood absolutely rigid. She blushed, looked down and said hello. My right hand whispered the same, then twitched and spun around. It slipped from the end of my arm like a leaf from a bough. She asked how I had been. My feet clattered off in opposite directions. I smiled and asked her how she had been. Before she might answer anything social and ordinary, a groan flew up my throat. My teeth couldn't resist its force and it was suddenly in the air. Both of us marveled, though I more than she. She was too polite to make anything of it and suggested we stroll. The groan hovered behind us, growing smaller and more contorted. While she talked of the last few months, I nodded at things I approved of. I approved of everything and nodded without cease until my head fell off. She looked away as I groped for it on the ground and put it back on, shouting hello, hello.

How could I have been so blind, so careless, cruel and stupid? This was a lovely girl. I, beast and fool, adjusting my head, felt now what I should have felt then. And I felt that Henry was marvelous. "Seen any movies lately?" I asked.

She stuttered something about a movie and Henry's impressions of it. The stutter was worse than I remembered, and now that I looked her face seemed thin, the flesh gray. In her effort not to stutter, strain showed in her neck. As if it were my habitual right, I took her hand. She continued to stutter something Henry had said about the movie, and didn't snap her hand back. Tears formed in my nose. "Thank you," I whispered. "F-for what?" she asked. We were near an empty lot. I turned abruptly against her, my lips quivering. She said, "Really, Phillip, I d-don't w-want . . ." With a rapid hand I discovered that she wore no underpants. We fell together. I caught sight of her later as she sprinted into the darkness. Groans issued from my mouth. They flew after her like a flock of bats.

It was a week before Henry came to see me, but I was certain I had heard the bell a hundred times. Each time, I put out my cigarette and dragged to the door, ready for a punch in the face, a knife or a bullet. In the middle of the night, I found myself sitting up in bed, my eyes large and compendious with dark as I shouted, "No, Henry, no." Though I shouted, I had resolved to say nothing or little when he finally came. Not a word would shape my mouth if I could help it. A word would be an excuse. Even self-denunciation was beyond decent possibility. If he flung acid in my face, I would fall and say, "Thanks." If he were out in the hall with a gun and fired point blank into my stomach, I might, as I toppled, blood sloshing through my lips, beg forgiveness. Though I merited no such opportunity, I hoped there would be time for it. If I could, while begging, keep my eyes fixed on him, it would be nice.

After three days passed and he still hadn't come, I thought of hanging myself. I tied a rope to the light bulb, made a noose and set a chair under it. But I couldn't, when I experimented, manage to open the door and then dash to the chair and hang myself without looking clumsy, as if I were really asking to be stopped. On the other hand, I didn't want to practice, become graceful and look effete. I considered poison: open the door, hello, down it goes, goodbye. Or fire: set myself on fire and shrivel, spitting curses on my head.

Despite all this I slept well most of the week, and on several nights I dreamed of Marjorie. We did it everytime. "Is this the nature of sin?" I asked. "This is nature," she said. "Don't talk." I discovered a truth in these dreams: each of my feelings was much like another, pity like lust, hate like love, sorrow like joy. I wondered if there were people who could keep them neat. I supposed not. They were feelings and not to be managed. If I felt bad I felt good. That was that.

The idea made me smile. When I noticed myself smiling, I chuckled a bit, and soon I was cackling. Tears streamed out of my eyes. I had to lie on the floor to keep from sinking there. I lay for a long time digging my nails into my cheeks and thought about the nature of ideas. Pascal, Plato, Freud. I felt kin to men like that. Having ideas, seized as it were. I had had an idea.

When I heard the doorbell I knew immediately that I had heard it. The ring was different from the phony ringing during the week. It was substantial, moral, piercing. It set me running to answer, dashing between tables and chairs, leaping a sofa, lunging down the hall to come flying to the ringing door where I swerved and came back to where I had been. A voice more primitive than any noise the body makes, said:

"Let the son of a bitch ring."

My lips slid up my teeth, my ears flattened to the skull. I found myself crouching. Muscles bunched in my shoulders. I felt a shuddering stiffness in my thighs. Tight as bow strings, tendons curled the bones of my hands to claws. The bell continued to ring, and a hot, ragged tongue slapped across my muzzle. I smelled the sweet horror of my breath. It bristled my neck and sent me gliding low to the ringing door, a noiseless animal, blacker and more secret than night.

Henry out there stood dying in his shoes, ringing in gruesome demise. My paws lifted and lopped down softly. Blood poured me, slow as steaming tar, inevitably toward the door. My paw lay on the knob. It turned. I tugged. Nothing happened. He rang. I shouted, "Can't open it. Give a shove." I tugged, Henry shoved. I twisted the knob and he flung himself against the other side. A panel dislodged. I had a glimpse of his face, feverish and shining. A blaze of white teeth cut the lower half. The door stayed shut. We yelled to one another.

"All right. Give it everything."

"Here we go."

The door opened.

Henry stood in the hall, looking straight into my eyes. The crooked nose, the blue eyes. The physical man. Nothing I felt, absolutely nothing, could accommodate the fact of him. I wondered if it were actually Henry, and I looked rapidly about his face, casting this and that aside like a man fumbling through his wallet for his driver's license while the trooper grimly waits. Nothing turned up to name him Henry. Even the familiar tooth left me unimpressed. Henry's features made no more sense than a word repeated fifty times. The physical man, Henry, Henry, Henry, Henry. Nothing. I wanted to cry and beg him to be Henry again, but only snickered and stepped back. He came inside. I took a package of cigarettes from my pocket and offered it to him. He stared, then shook his head. The movement was trivial, but it was no. No! It startled me into sense. I put the cigarettes back into my pocket and sighed. The breath ran out slowly, steadily, like sand through an hour glass. This was it. He followed with a sigh of his own, then said, "I guess this is it."

"I guess," I murmured, "it is."

"Yes," he said, "it is," and took a long, deep breath, as if drawing up the air I had let out.

I began to strangle. Neither of us spoke. I coughed. He cleared his throat in a sympathetic reflex. I coughed. He cleared his throat once more. I coughed a third time, and he waited for me to stop, but I continued to cough. I was barely able to see, though my eyes bulged. He asked if I wanted a glass of water. I nodded and doubled forward wiping my bulging eyes. When he returned with the water I seized it and drank. He asked if I wanted another glass. I said, "No thanks," coughed again, a rasping, rotten-chested hack. He rushed for another glass. I saw it trembling in his hand. His sleeve was wet to the elbow. "Thanks," I said and seized it.

"Go on, go on, drink."

I drank.

"Finish it," he urged.

I finished it slowly.

"You ought to sit down."

I went to a chair and sat down. My head rolled in a dull, feeble way, and a moment passed in silence. Then he said:

"There has been enough of this."

I stood up instantly.

He looked at me hard. I tried to look back

equally hard, as if his look were an order that I do the same. His height and sharp little eyes gave him the advantage. "Yes," I said, shaking my head yes.

"Months of it. Enough!"

"I'm responsible," I muttered, and that put force into my look. "All my fault," I said, force accumulating.

"Don't be ridiculous. I don't blame you for anything. You want to kill me and I don't blame you for that. I'm no friend. I betrayed you."

"Kill you?"

"I came here expecting death. I am determined to settle for nothing less."

"Don't be absurd."

"Absurd? Is it so absurd to want justice? Is it so absurd to ask the friend one has betrayed to do for one the only possible thing that will purge one?"

He moved an inch closer and seemed to be restraining himself, with terrific difficulty, from moving closer.

"Shut up, Henry," I said. "I have no intention of killing you and I never wanted to do such a thing."

"Ha! I see now."

"You don't see a thing, Henry."

"I see," he shouted and slapped his head. "I see why you refuse to do it, why you pretend you don't even want to do it."

[6 4]

He slapped his head again very hard.

"I see, Phillip, you're a moral genius. By not killing me you administer cruel, perfect justice."

"Henry, get a hold of yourself. Be fair to both of us, will you."

"Don't hand me that liberal crap, Phillip. Don't talk to me about fair. You be fair. Do the right thing, the merciful thing. Kill me, Phillip."

I started backing toward the door, my hands stuffed deep between my lowest ribs. Henry shuffled after me, his little eyes wild with fury and appreciation. "No use. I will follow you until you show mercy. I will bring you guns and knives and ropes, vats of poison, acids, gasoline and matches. I will leap in front of your car. I will . . ."

Whirling suddenly, I was out the door. Henry gasped and followed, tearing for a grip on the back of my head. We went down the night, Henry ripping out fists of my flying hair and jamming them into his mouth so he might choke. The night became day, and day night. These a week, the week a month. My hair was soon gone from the back of my head. When it grew in he ripped it out again. The wind lacerated our faces and tore the clothes off our bodies. Occasionally, I heard him scream, "I have a gun. Shoot me." Or, "A rope, Phillip. Strangle me." I had a step on him always and I ran on powerful legs. Over the running years, they grew more powerful. They stretched and swelled to the size of trees while my body shrank and my head descended. At last my arms disappeared and I was a head on legs. Running.

The Deal

TWENTY WERE JAMMED TOGETHER ON THE stoop; tiers of heads made one central head, and the wings rested along the banisters: a raggedy monster of boys studying her approach. Her white face and legs. She passed without looking, poked her sunglasses against the bridge of her nose and tucked her bag between her arm and ribs. She carried it at her hip like a rifle stock. On her spine forty eyes hung like poison berries. Bone dissolved beneath her lank beige silk, and the damp circle of her belt cut her in half. Independent legs struck toward the points of her shoes. Her breasts lifted and rode the air like porpoises. She would cross to the grocery as usual, buy cigarettes, then cross back despite their eyes. As if the neighborhood hadn't changed one bit. She slipped the bag forward to crack it against her belly and pluck out keys and change. In the gesture she was home from work. Her keys jangled in the sun as if they opened everything and the air received her. The monster, watching, saw the glove fall away.

Pigeons looped down to whirl between buildings, and a ten-wheel truck came slowly up the street. As it passed she emerged from the grocery, then stood at the curb opposite the faces. She glanced along the street where she had crossed it. No glove. Tar reticulated between the cobbles. A braid of murky water ran against the curb, twisting bits of flotsam toward the drain. She took off her sunglasses, dropped them with her keys into the bag, then stepped off the curb toward the faces. Addressing them with a high, friendly voice, she said: "Did you guys see a glove? I dropped it a moment ago."

The small ones squinted up at her from the bottom step. On the middle steps sat boys fourteen or fifteen years old. The oldest ones made the wings. Dandies and introverts, they sprawled, as if with a common corruption in their bones. In the center, his eyes level with hers, a boy waited for her attention in the matter of gloves. To his right sat a very thin boy with a pocked face. A narrow-brimmed hat tipped

toward his nose and shaded the continuous activity
of his eyes. She spoke to the green eyes of the boy in
the center and held up the glove she had: "Like this."

Teeth appeared below the hat, then everywhere
as the boys laughed. Did she hold up a fish? Green
eyes said: "Hello, Miss Calile."

She looked around at the faces, then laughed
with them at her surprise. "You know my name?"

"I see it on the mailbox," said the hat. "He can't
read. I see it."

"My name is Duke Francisco," said the illiterate.

"My name is Abbe Carlyle," she said to him.

The hat smirked. "His name Francisco Lopez."

Green eyes turned to the hat. "Shut you mouth,
baby. I tell her my name, not you."

"His name Francisco Lopez," the hat repeated.

She saw pocks and teeth, the thin oily face and
the hat, as he spoke again, nicely to her: "My name
Francisco Pacheco, the Prince. I seen you name on
the mailbox."

"Did either of you . . ."

"You name is shit," said green eyes to the hat.

"My name is Tito." A small one on the bottom
step looked up for the effect of his name. She looked
down at him. "I am Tito," he said.

"Did you see my glove, Tito?"

"This is Tomato," he answered, unable to bear her attention. He nudged the boy to his left. Tomato nudged back, stared at the ground.

"I am happy to know you, Tito," she said, "and you, Tomato. Both of you." She looked back up to green eyes and the hat. The hat acknowledged her courtesy. He tilted back to show her his eyes, narrow and black except for bits of white reflected in the corners. His face was thin, high-boned and fragile. She pitied the riddled skin.

"This guy," he said, pointing his thumb to the right, "is Monkey," and then to the left beyond green eyes, "and this guy is Beans." She nodded to the hat, then Monkey, then Beans, measuring the respect she offered, doling it out in split seconds. Only one of them had the glove.

"Well, did any of you guys see my glove?"

Every tier grew still, like birds in a tree waiting for a sign that would move them all at once.

Tito's small dark head snapped forward. She heard the slap an instant late. The body lurched after the head and pitched off the stoop at her feet. She saw green eyes sitting back slowly. Tito gaped up at her from the concrete. A sacrifice to the lady. She stepped back as if rejecting it and frowned at green eyes. He gazed indifferently at Tito, who was up, facing him with coffee-bean fists. Tito screamed, "I tell her you got it, dick-head."

The green eyes swelled in themselves like a light blooming in the ocean. Tito's fists opened, he turned, folded quickly and sat back into the mass. He began to rub his knees.

"May I have my glove, Francisco?" Her voice was still pleasant and high. She now held her purse in the crook of her arm and pressed it against her side.

Some fop had a thought and giggled in the wings. She glanced up at him immediately. He produced a toothpick. With great delicacy he stuck it into his ear. She looked away. Green eyes again waited for her. A cup of darkness formed in the hollow that crowned his chestbone. His soiled gray polo shirt hooked below it. "You think I have you glove?" She didn't answer. He stared between his knees, between heads and shoulders to the top of Tito's head. "Hey, Tito, you tell her I got the glove?"

"I didn't tell nothing," muttered Tito rubbing his knees harder as if they were still bitter from his fall.

"He's full of shit, Miss Calile. I break his head later. What kind of glove you want?"

"This kind," she said wearily, "a white glove like this."

"Too hot." He grinned.

"Yes, too hot, but I need it."

"What for? Too hot." He gave her full green concern.

"It's much too hot, but the glove is mine, mister."

She rested her weight on one leg and wiped her brow with the glove she had. They watched her do it, the smallest of them watched her, and she moved the glove slowly to her brow again and drew it down her cheek and neck. She could think of nothing to say, nothing to do without expressing impatience. Green eyes changed the subject. "You live there." He pointed toward her building.

"That's right."

A wooden front door with a window in it showed part of the shadowy lobby, mailboxes, and a second door. Beyond her building and down the next street were warehouses. Beyond them, the river. A meat truck started toward them from a packing house near the river. It came slowly, bug-eyed with power. The driver saw the lady standing in front of the boys. He yelled as the truck went past. Gears yowled, twisting the sound of his voice. She let her strength out abruptly: "Give me the glove, Francisco."

The boy shook his head at the truck, at her lack of civilization. "What you give me?"

That tickled the hat. "*Vaya,* baby. What she give you, eh?" He spoke fast, his tone decorous and filthy.

"All right, baby," she said fast as the hat, "what do you want?" The question had New York and much man in it. The hat swiveled to the new sound. A man of honor, let him understand the terms. He squinted at her beneath the hat brim.

"Come on, Francisco, make your deal." She presented brave, beautiful teeth, smiling hard as a skull.

"Tell her, Duke. Make the deal." The hat lingered on "deal," grateful to the lady for this word.

The sun shone in his face and the acknowledged duke sat dull, green eyes blank with possibilities. Her question, not "deal," held him. It had come too hard, too fast. He laughed in contempt of something and glanced around at the wings. They offered nothing. "I want a dollar," he said.

That seemed obvious to the hat: he sneered, "He wants a dollar." She had to be stupid not to see it.

"No deal. Twenty-five cents." Her gloves were worth twenty dollars. She had paid ten for them at a sale. At the moment they were worth green eyes' life.

"I want ten dollars," said green eyes flashing the words like extravagant meaningless things; gloves of his own. He lifted his arms, clasped his hands behind his head and leaned against the knees behind him. His belly filled with air, the polo shirt rolled out on its curve. He made a fat man doing business. "Ten dollars." Ten fingers popped up behind his head like grimy spikes. Keeper of the glove, cocky duke of the stoop. The number made him happy: it bothered her. He drummed the spikes against his head: "I wan' you ten dol-lar." Beans caught the beat in his hips and rocked it on the stoop.

"Francisco," she said, hesitated, then said, "dig me, please. You will get twenty-five cents. Now let's have the glove." Her bag snapped open, her fingers hooked, stiffened on the clasp. Monkey leered at her and bongoed his knees with fists. "The number is ten dol-lar." She waited, said nothing. The spikes continued drumming, Monkey rocked his hips, Beans pummeled his knees. The hat sang sadly: "Twany fyiv not d'nummer, not d'nummer, not d'nummer." He made claves of his fingers and palms, tocked, clicked his tongue against the beat. "Twan-ny fyiv— na t'nomma." She watched green eyes. He was quiet now in the center of the stoop, sitting motionless, waiting, as though seconds back in time his mind still touched the question: what did he want? He seemed to wonder, now that he had the formula, what *did* he want? The faces around him, dopey in the music, wondered nothing, grinned at her, nodded, clicked, whined the chorus: "Twany fyiv not t'nomma, twany fyiv not t'nomma."

Her silk blouse stained and stuck flat to her breasts and shoulders. Water chilled her sides.

"Ten dol-lar iss t'nomma."

She spread her feet slightly, taking better possession of the sidewalk and resting on them evenly, the bag held open for green eyes. She could see he didn't want that, but she insisted in her silence he did. Tito spread his little feet and lined the points of his shoes against hers. Tomato noticed the imitation and cackled at the concrete. The music went on, the beat feeding on itself, pulverizing words, smearing them into liquid submission: "Iss t'nomma twany fyiv? Dat iss not t'nomma."

"Twenty-five cents," she said again.

Tito whined, "Gimme twenty-five cents."

"Shut you mouth," said the hat, and turned a grim face to his friend. In the darkness of his eyes there were deals. The music ceased. "Hey, baby, you got no manners? Tell what you want." He spoke in a dreamy voice, as if to a girl.

"I want a kiss," said green eyes.

She glanced down with this at Tito and studied the small shining head. "Tell him to give me my glove, Tito," she said cutely, nervously. The wings shuffled and looked down bored. Nothing was happening. Twisting backwards Tito shouted up to green eyes, "Give her the glove." He twisted front again and crouched over his knees. He shoved Tomato for approval and smiled. Tomato shoved him back, snarled at the concrete and spit between his feet at a face which had taken shape in the grains.

"I want a kiss," said the boy again.

She sighed, giving another second to helplessness. The sun was low above the river and the street three quarters steeped in shade. Sunlight cut across the building tops where pigeons swept by loosely and fluttered in to pack the stone foliage of the eaves. Her bag snapped shut. Her voice was business: "Come on, Francisco. I'll give you the kiss."

He looked shot among the faces.

"Come on," she said, "it's a deal."

The hat laughed out loud with childish insanity. The others shrieked and jiggled, except for the wings. But they ceased to sprawl, and seemed to be getting bigger, to fill with imminent motion. "Gimme a kiss, gimme a kiss," said the little ones on the lowest step. Green eyes sat with a quiet, open mouth.

"Let's go," she said. "I haven't all day."

"Where I go?"

"That doorway." She pointed to her building and

took a step toward it. "You know where I live, don't
you?"

"I don't want no kiss."

"What's the matter now?"

"You scared?" asked the hat. "Hey, Duke, you
scared?"

The wings leaned toward the center, where
green eyes hugged himself and made a face.

"Look, Mr. Francisco, you made a deal."

"Yeah," said the wings.

"Now come along."

"I'm not scared," he shouted and stood up
among them. He sat down. "I don't want no kiss."

"You're scared?" she said.

"You scared chicken," said the hat.

"Yeah," said the wings. "Hey, punk. Fairy. Hey,
Duke Chicken."

"Duke scared," mumbled Tito. Green eyes stood
up again. The shoulders below him separated. Tito
leaped clear of the stoop and trotted into the street.
Green eyes passed through the place he had vacated
and stood at her side, his head not so high as her
shoulder. She nodded at him, tucked her bag up and
began walking toward her building. A few others
stood up on the stoop and the hat started down. She
turned. "Just him." Green eyes shuffled after her. The

hat stopped on the sidewalk. Someone pushed him forward. He resisted, but called after them, "He's my cousin." She walked on, the boy came slowly after her. They were yelling from the stoop, the hat yelling his special point, "He's my brother." He stepped after them and the others swarmed behind him down the stoop and onto the sidewalk. Tito jumped out of the street and ran alongside the hat. He yelled, "He's got the glove." They all moved down the block, the wings trailing sluggishly, the young ones jostling, punching each other, laughing, shrieking things in Spanish after green eyes and the lady. She heard him, a step behind her. "I give you the glove and take off."

She put her hand out to the side a little. The smaller hand touched hers and took it. "You made a deal."

She tugged him through the doorway into the tight, square lobby. The hand snapped free and he swung by, twisting to face her as if to meet a blow. He put his back against the second door, crouched a little. His hands pressed the sides of his legs. The front door shut slowly and the shadows deepened in the lobby. He crouched lower, his eyes level with her breasts, as she took a step toward him. The hat appeared, a black rock in the door window. Green eyes saw it, straightened up, one hand moving quickly toward his pants pocket. The second and third head, thick dark bulbs, lifted beside the hat in the window. Bodies piled against the door behind her. Green eyes held up the glove. "Here, you lousy glove."

She smiled and put out her hand. The hat screamed, "Hey, you made a deal, baby. Hey, you got no manners."

"Don't be scared," she whispered, stepping closer.

The glove lifted toward her and hung in the air between them, gray, languid as smoke. She took it and bent toward his face. "I won't kiss you. Run." The window went black behind her, the lobby solid in darkness, silent but for his breathing, the door breathing against the pressure of the bodies, and the scraping of fingers spread about them like rats in the walls. She felt his shoulder, touched the side of his neck, bent the last inch and kissed him. White light cut the walls. They tumbled behind it, screams and bright teeth. Spinning to face them she was struck, pitched against green eyes and the second door. He twisted hard, shoved away from her as the faces piled forward popping eyes and lights, their fingers accumulating in the air, coming at her. She raised the bag, brought it down swishing into the faces, and wrenched and twisted to get free of the fingers, screaming against their shrieks, "Stop it, stop it, stop it." The bag sprayed papers and coins, and the sunglasses flew over their heads and cracked against the brass mailboxes. She dropped amid shrieks, "Gimme a kiss, gimme a kiss," squirming down the door onto her knees to get fingers out from under her and she thrust up with the bag into bellies and thighs until a fist banged her mouth. She cursed, flailed at nothing.

There was light in the lobby and leather scraping on concrete as they crashed out the door into the street. She shut her eyes instantly as the fist came again, big as her face. Then she heard running in the street. The lobby was silent. The door shut slowly, the shadows deepened. She could feel the darkness getting thicker. She opened her eyes. Standing in front of her was the hat.

He bowed slightly. "I get those guys for you. They got no manners." The hat shook amid the shadows, slowly, sadly.

She pressed the smooth leather of her bag against her cheek where the mouths had kissed it. Then she tested the clasp, snapping it open and shut. The hat shifted his posture and waited. "You hit me," she whispered and did not look up at him. The hat bent and picked up her keys and the papers. He handed the keys to her, then the papers, and bent again for the coins. She dropped the papers into her bag and stuffed them together in the bottom. "Help me up!" She took his hands and got to her feet without looking at him. As she put the key against the lock of the second door she began to shiver. The key rattled against the slot. "Help me!" The hat leaned over the lock, his long thin fingers squeezing the key. It caught, angled with a click. She pushed him aside. "You give me something? Hey, you give me something?" The door shut on his voice.

Intimations

MAMMA WAS COMING. SARAH WAS STIFF AND
pale. Myron walked circles saying chicken chow
mein. If Mamma asks say chicken chow mein.
There was a knock. Sarah said chicken chow mein,
opened the door. Mamma. Stockings rolled in rubber bands just below the knees. She had something
for them in a shopping bag: lox, rye bread, salami,
chocolate cake. . . . Then it was five A.M. Light
hung about their heads like iron. Naked, staring at
Myron, Sarah was poignant with the need to pee.
Myron talked about pain, Sarah, and the need we
must feel, Sarah, to accept pain. Yet he had suffered
doubts. He had been less than cool. Indeed, shikse
blonde or purple eggplant, she was his wife and had
made a delicious dinner. Mistake or not, Sarah. Yet

he'd been doubtful when he said, if Mamma asks
—which she did—say chicken chow mein—which
they did. He'd been doubtful when Mamma was
eating it, pork casserole, but he babbled distractions
and filled the wineglass from which she drank nothing, Sarah, because she was eating misgivings away
—hers and theirs, Sarah. And yet in the loving mo-
mentum of Mamma's teeth didn't everything seem
fine, Sarah, hugging goodbye, gimme-a-call, Sarah.
Then the door was locked, Sarah, and Mamma was
in the subway tunneling out of mind and he took
Sarah, Sarah, and stripped her like a twig and came
trip hammers and sprawled all bones until the
phone rang weirdly oh god, Sarah. And a hideous
bird voice said Mamma had had a trichinol seizure
and he screamed filthyfuckingmiddlewesternswine-
peddlers, Sarah, waking, to stare at Sarah's gray
eyes staring at him out of sleep and nightmare. I'm
talking about pain, Sarah. How the old must suffer,
Sarah, because we grow, we change, and we honor
them, Sarah, by acknowledging and making clear
to ourselves that we accept life's inexorable sophistication and cruel, natural, inevitable growing away
from primitive intimations of kindness, Sarah, and
the phone rang. From the bathroom she yelled acknowledge it, Myron. And it rang, Myron.

Making Changes

THE HALL WAS CLOGGED WITH BODIES; NONE OF them hers, but who could be sure? The light was bad, there was too much noise, too much movement. Too many people had been invited. More kept arriving. I liked it, but it was hard to get from one room to another. Conversation was impossible. People had to lean close and shriek. It killed the effect of wit, looking into nostrils, shrieking, "What? What?" But it was a New York scene. I liked it. Except she was missing; virtually torn out of my hands. Cecily. I would have asked people if they had seen her, but I was ashamed to admit I had lost her. I was afraid she was someone's date or inextricably into something. I was afraid she was copulating. She had been dressed, but it was a New

York scene. Minutes had passed. I shoved through
the hall—hot, dark, squealing with bodies—and
looked for her. I shoved into the kitchen and saw
just one couple, a lady in a brown tweed suit talking to a short dapper man in spats. She was stout,
fiftyish, had fierce eyes. Flat, black as nailheads.
Her voice flew around like pots and pans. The man
glanced at me, then down as if embarrassed. The
lady ignored me. I ignored her and busied around
the wet, sloppy counter looking for an unused glass
and a bottle of something, as if I wanted a drink.
The lady was saying, slam, clang:

"Sexual enlightenment, the keystone of modern-
ity, I dare say, can hardly be considered an atavistic
intellectual debauch, Cosmo."

"But the perversions . . ."

"To be sure, the perversions of which we are so
richly conscious are the natural inclination, indeed
the style, of civilized beings."

I found a paper cup. It was gnawed about the
rim, but no cigarettes were shredding on the bottom.
I sloshed in bourbon and started to leave, afraid she
was pervulating.

"Wait there, you."

I stopped.

"What sort of pervert are you?"

I shrugged, mumbled, hoping she'd forgo.

"What sort of pervert are you?"

I shrugged, mumbled.

"Speak up, fellow."

"I mug yaks."

"You hear, Cosmo? A yak mugger."

"Are you married, young man?" asked Cosmo, dreamily.

"No."

"Good question," she cried, "for we observe, as necessarily we must, that marriage encourages perversity—assuming the parties agree on specified indulgences, Cosmo, which is paradoxical."

"Indeed, Tulip, the natural perversions themselves, one might well assume," he said, whispering.

"Let me continue."

"Please, please do."

Something shadowy and mean in her voice wanted to spring, to rip off his head. I wanted to leave.

"Let me continue."

"Please, please do."

"Paradoxical, I repeat, for the prime value of sex, to an advanced view, lies precisely in its antagonism to society. What, then, dare one ask, must we make of marriage?"

"An anti-social perversion," he said.

"Yes, clearly," I added, "clearly."

The words burst out of themselves with a wonderful feeling. I love logic. Its inevitability, its power of consummation.

"Cosmo," she said, ignoring me, "you're a horse's ass."

She looked at me. I nodded my head. "Clearly."

"I say, fellow, is much going on in the living room?" Her black eyes, like periods, stopped mine.

"I just came the other way, actually. From the back of the apartment."

I pointed.

"How fascinating. Do publish a travel book. In the meantime, look behind you."

I turned and looked through the dining room over scattered struggling to the living room. It was piled and dense with sluggish, sliding spaghetti.

"It's mainly in there now." I pointed.

"Good. The orgy, Cosmo, our oldest mode of sexual community has moved closer. Let's go watch now that we needn't poke about the rooms like vulgar tourists. Oh, Cosmo, what better solvent have we for the diversity of human beings? And, needless to add, it's such a chic way of breaking the ice."

They left the kitchen, her smashing voice flinging in all directions, and hesitated at the edge of the toiling pile with spray in their eyes. Figures cast up like tidal garbage lay quivering at their feet.

"Cosmo, the view is breathtaking. Tell me your impressions."

"Breathtaking, a view of the infinite mind. Indeed, the mind, that ocean where each kind . . ."

"Yes, yes . . . where every sort its own sort shortly finds."

I pushed by them down the edge of the mind, squatting, peering at whatever caught light—blades, nails, paps, hips, tips—looking for her blond hair, her grey eyes, her legs.

I pushed beyond the mind, back into the clogged hall, and looked into a bedroom. Three mirrors showed me looking. I went on, looked into a study and saw a wall of whips, barbells on the floor, framed diplomas, photos of movie stars and contemporary philosophers. I found a bathroom. I knocked, stepped in. A naked man sitting pertly in the tub said, "I'll bet you're Zeus. I'm Danaë." I shook my head, backed out muttering, "I'm Phillip." Again in the hall, rump to rump, hip to hip, between moaning, writhing walls; pardon me, so so sorry, until a knee plugged under my crotch and I pitched to a side and down elbow deep in churning, hands smack on a hot face. Eyes gleamed through my fingers, teeth nibbled my palm, fingers clapped my thigh, squeezed to nerve and my fist swung back like a hoof. Struck neck. "You want to hit?" There was a punch, a slap, a gibbering girl tumbling over me and nails raked my spine. I scrambled for space, slammed nose flat into shivering thighs, pinwheeled, flapped cha cha cha like a sheet in the wind, and fell out against bare wall, wheezing, whistling into virtual black. Tulip's voice slashed it like tracers:

"I will say one thing, Cosmo, you meet people in an orgy. Not like conventional sex, sneaking in corners, undermining human society, selfish, acquisitive, dirty. I mean every time one gets laid, as it were, it's conservative politics, don't you think? On the other hand, orgies are liberal, humane. The ambience of impulse, the deluge of sensation, why orgies are corporate form, the highest expression of our catholicity, our modern escape from constrictive, compulsive, unilinear simplifications of medieval sex. Don't you think?"

"They give me a certain cultural feeling."

People were sliding across my legs.

"Precisely."

A pulsing hole went by.

"Precisely a feeling of mind, as it were."

People were sliding across my legs like lizards. I was inching one buttock at a time toward the foyer. A squeal of recognition needled my ear. My hands flew up, slapped a breast, belly, weedy groove.

"You!"

She collapsed into my arms and we went sliding down the molding like snakes, sliding out of massy sucking foliage. But she quit, suddenly dead as a ton. I dragged. She babbled encouragement, "Gimme, gimme sincere." I reached the door with her, opened it, and light swept her body. Bruised, vaporous, shining with oils, more limp than any deposition I'd ever seen, more tragic than Cordelia in the arms of Lear. But she wasn't Cecily.

She was all right. Whoever she was, squalid enervation made easy lines like vines; lips, like avocado pulp, hung lovey in her face. Nose, belly, legs, all in good repair. I helped her stand, then turned her about to consider another prospect. I smiled. She smiled. Both of us a smidgeon self-conscious, confronting one another this way, a couple in the eyes of the world, standing apart, she and I, and it wasn't easy to think, to ignore the great pull of the worm bucket and pretend to individuation. She gave way shyly under my glance, and leaned toward the wall. There was no wall. Her hands flailed like shot ducks, her eyes grabbed for mine, flashing fright and dismay, and I flung after her into the sticky dismal, thrashing, groping like Beowulf in the mere for a grip on Grendel. I seized a wrist. I dragged, dragged us up to light. She whimpered so at the injustice, the imbecilic ironies. For her sake I contained my own distress. It wasn't exactly she. Like her, like her in many ways. Not a speck worse. But another girl. I released her, simpered an apology.

"You must love me very much," she said. "My name is Nora."

Such tender imperative. Another time, another place, who knows what might have been. If circumstances were slightly different, the light better, noise a little less, if, if, if I hadn't shoved her back in, furious with myself, we might have had a moment, a life . . .

"To think, Cosmo, how we build on merest chance—marriage, society, great societies—as if there weren't ever so much to choose from, so much that any choice at all must seem fanatical in its limitation. Isn't it that which makes the satyr frightfully amusing, his perpetual hard on?"

"Ho, ho. A singular notion. But awfully true, Tulip. Awfully true, indeed."

I stumbled past them at the titillating margin. She was mushing his little rear in her fist.

"Cosmo, Cosmo, I think I see a perversion. You'll have to tell me what it's called. If only there were a bit more light. My, how it smells. Cosmo, what would you call that smell? The vocabulary of olfaction is so limited in English."

"Communism?"

"I adore your political intelligence, Cosmo. Why is it on every other subject you're such a horse's ass?"

I shoved into a bathroom to wash and look for fungicide, slammed the door, flicked the light. *Voilà!* A girl. She was bent over the sink having spasms. I pressed beside her, ran the water, snapped a towel off the rack.

"May I?"

She presented her chin, flecked, runny as it was, and didn't make an occasion of it. Her eyes were full of tears. Elegant grey eyes like hers; blond hair to the shoulders, in love with gravity. In less than a minute there was a bond, soft and strong as silk, holding us. I wiped her chin, we laughed at nothing, chatted, smoked a cigarette, and felt embarrassed by our luck in each other. I peed and one of us said, "Let's get out of this party," and the other said, "Yes, right now." Holding hands tightly we left the bathroom and worked down the hall and through the living room. More people were arriving, thickening the stew; dull raging continued all around. At the door stood a big man.

"I'm glad you came tonight, Harold."

"I'm glad you're glad," I said. "Name is Stanley."

He wore a shirt and tie, nothing else. He had bloodshot eyes, a beard, a cigar in his mouth. Fumes drifted from his nostrils as if from boiling sinuses.

"I'm sorry you're leaving."

"I'm sorry you're sorry."

"I feel as if you want to say something nasty to me, Harold."

"Not at all, I assure you."

His legs were black and wild with hair. Burning meat looped on his thigh.

"You must have had a fight with one of your girlfriends. And I have to pay for it, eh Harold? Well, what's a fuck'n friend for if you can't mutilate him every ten minutes, eh?"

He laughed, winked at her.

I edged by him, nodding agreeably, grinning, slapping his shoulder lightly. Not too intimate. I knew the signs and wanted to give no excuse for violence. I tugged her along behind me into the outside hall. He leaned after us, saying, "How do you like my beard, Harold?"

"Makes you look religious."

"You think I'm not religious?"

"I mean it's a nice religious beard."

"Say what you mean, Harold. I hate innuendo. I'm not religious. I'm Satan, right? What should I do, Harold?"

He was yelling as we went through the lobby, then out to the street. She squeezed my hand, pressed to my side. He pressed to my other side, yelling, "A moralist like you knows about people. I'd like to be like you and keep my principles intact, but I'm weak, Harold. I lack integrity. I haven't the courage to commit suicide, Harold."

He laughed, nudged my ribs with a big fist. His meat angered and there were suddenly two of him: Laughing and Angry. I snickered and looked up the street for a cab. She whispered, "Ignore him," and I whispered, "Good idea." I saw a cab, waved. It started toward us. She got right in, but he had my arm now.

"Wait one minute, Harold. I want your opinion about a moral problem."

He pushed his face at mine and tapped his beard, grinning and winking. "Which way is better, pointed or rounded?"

"How about growing it into your mouth?"

He let go of me and stepped back.

"That would kill our conversation, Harold. And you know when people stop talking they start fighting. For instance, if I stopped talking right now I might kick you in the nuts."

He stopped talking, dropped his hands lightly on his hips, spread his legs. I kicked him in the nuts.

"Ooch."

I leaped into the cab, slammed the door, slammed the lock, and his face smeared the window as I rolled it up. His eyes glazed, his upper lip shriveled, spit came bubbling between his teeth. His fingers clawed then whipped across the glass as the cab shot away. I turned to her. She was staring at me with big lights in her eyes, quivering. She dropped her eyes. I inhaled, rubbed my hands together to keep them from shaking and from touching her.

"That look on his face," I said.

"And his penis."

"That, too."

"It was so biblical."

"Old Testament."

She touched me, then took my hand. Going across town we talked about the people, what they looked like, what they said, who did what and so on. We talked in my apartment, listened to our voices, boats in the river, planes in the sky, and it was impossible to say when it happened or who laid whom and we fell asleep too soon afterwards to think about it. Not that I would have thought about it. I'm not a poet, I'm Phillip. And then I awoke as if from a nightmare and it was brilliant morning. She was standing like a stork on one leg, pulling a stocking up the other. She said, "Hello," and her voice was full of welcome, but I saw she was too much in motion, already someplace else. Her eyes were pleasant, but they looked through mine as if mine weren't eyes, just tunnels that zoomed out the back of my head.

"Leaving?"

"I'll call you later. What's your number?"

"Leaving?"

I stared at her. She finished dressing, then sat stiffly on the bed to say goodbye. We kissed. It was external for her. I seized her arms, kissed harder, deeper. She was all surface despite me, despite the way she felt to me. I released her.

"Look," I said, "you can't leave."

"Please, Phillip. It's been nice, very nice."

She stared at a wall.

"Is something the matter?"

"No."

A toilet flushed next door, water retched in pipes. I got out of bed and went naked to my desk. I found a pen, returned, and pushed her backwards onto the bed.

"I'm all dressed, Phillip."

I shook her hands off, lifted her dress, and scribbled across her belly: PHILLIP'S. On her thighs: PHILLIP'S, PHILLIP'S.

She sat up, considered herself, then me. As she rehooked her stockings she said, "Why do that?"

"I don't know."

"You must have something in mind."

"What can I say? I'm aware the couple is a lousy idea. I read books. I go to the flicks. I'm hip. I live in

New York. But I want you to come back. Will you come back?"

"I have a date."

"A what?"

"Can't I have a date? I made it before we met."

"Break it."

"No."

"Will you come back?"

"I'll try."

"Today?"

"I'll try," she said, straightened her dress, went to the door, out, and down the steps. D'gook, d'gook. The street door opened. She was gone. I was empty.

I flopped on the bed, picked up the phone, and called my date for the afternoon. A man answered.

"Yeah?"

"May I speak to Genevieve?"

"Hey, baby, the telephone."

His voice was heavy, slow, rotten with satisfaction. Heels clacked to the phone. A bracelet clicked, a cigarette sizzled, she exhaled, "Thanks Max," then, "Hello."

"This is Phillip."

"Phillip? Phillip, hello. I'm so happy you called. What time are you coming for me?"

"Never, bitch."

I dropped the phone, g'choonk.

I flopped on the bed, empty, listening to the phone ringing, ringing, and fell asleep before it stopped. There was no moment of silence, no dreaming, nothing but the sound of her footsteps going down, then coming up, a knock at the door and I awoke. It was early afternoon. She leaned over me.

"Phillip."

I caught her hand, dragged her down like a subaqueous evil scaly. We kissed. She kissed me. I bit her ear. We kissed and there was no outside except for the phone ringing again. I let it. We had D. H. Lawrence, Norman Mailer, *triste*.

I lighted cigarettes and put the ashtray on her belly. Even tired, groggy, *triste,* I could see we were a great team. Smoke bloomed, light failed, I savored the world. Before the room became dark I turned on my side to examine her belly and thighs. The PHILLIP'S were in each of the places. All about them like angry birds were: MAX'S, FRANK'S, HUGO'S, SIMON'S.

"For God's sake," I said.

I looked into her eyes, she mine. She put out her cigarette, gave me the ashtray, and turned her back to me. I was about to yell, but was stopped by writing down her spine: YOYO'S, MONKEY'S, HOMER'S, THE EIGHTY SEVENTH STREET SOCIAL AND ATHLETIC CLUB'S.

My voice trickled.

"All right, we'll do this properly. Get to know one another. I see you're difficult. Good. Difficulty is an excellent instructor, just the one I need. It'll extend the reach of my original impressions. I misjudged you, but I appreciate you. I'll study you like a course. Turn around. Let me kiss you, all right?"

She turned around. I kissed her. She kissed me. We had Henry Miller.

In the shower I scrubbed everyone off front and back and asked her name.

"Cecily," she said.

"I'm Phillip," I said, "but you knew that. Cecily? Of course, Cecily."

I couldn't have stopped the tears unless I'd chopped out my ducts with an adze. She giggled, stamped her feet, clapped her hands with glee.

Mildred

MILDRED WAS AT THE MIRROR ALL MORNING, cutting and shaping her hair. Then, every hour or so, she came up to me with her head tipped like this, like that, cheeks sucked in, a shine licked across her lips. I said, "Very nice," and finally I said, "Very, very nice."

"I'm not pretty."

"Yes; you're pretty."

"I know I'm attractive in a way, but basically I'm ugly."

"Your hair is very nice."

"Basically, I hate my type. When I was little I used to wish my name were Terry. Do you like my hair?"

"Your hair is very nice."

"I think you're stupid-looking."

"That's life."

"You're the only stupid-looking boyfriend I ever had. I've had stupid boyfriends, but none of them looked stupid. You look stupid."

"I like your looks."

"You're also incompetent, indifferent, a liar, a crook, and a coward."

"I like your looks."

"I was told that except for my nose my face is perfect. It's true."

"What's wrong with your nose?"

"I don't have to say it, Miller."

"What's wrong with it?"

"My nose, I've been told, is a millimeter too long. Isn't it?"

"I like your nose."

"Coward. I can forgive you for some things, but cowardice is unforgivable. And I'll get you for this, Miller. I'll make you cry."

"I like your legs."

"You're the only boyfriend I've ever had who was a coward. It's easy to like my legs."

"They're beautiful. I like both of them."

"Ha. Ha. What about my nose?"

"I'm crazy about your big nose."

"You dirty, fuck'n aardvark. What about yours, Miller? Tell me . . ."

The phone rang.

"His master's voice," she said and snatched it away from me. "Me, this time. Hello." She smacked it down.

"What was that about?"

"A man."

"What did he say?"

"Disgusting."

"What did he say?"

"He asked how much I charged . . . I don't care to talk about it."

"To what?"

"It was disgusting. I don't care to talk about it, understand. Answer the fuck'n phone yourself next time."

She dropped onto the bed. "Hideous."

"Did you recognize the voice?"

"I was humiliated."

"Tell me what he said."

"It must have been one of your stinking friends. I'm going to rip that phone out of the wall. Just hideous, hideous."

I lay down beside her.

"He asked how much I charged to suck assholes."

I shut my eyes.

"Did you hear what I said, Miller?"

"Big deal."

"I was humiliated."

"You can't stand intimacy."

"I'll rip out the phone if it happens once more. You can make your calls across the street in the bar."

"He was trying to say he loves you."

She thrashed into one position, then another, then another. I opened my eyes and said, "Let's play our game."

"No; I want to sleep."

"All right, lie still. I want to sleep, too."

"Then sleep."

I shut my eyes.

"I'll play once. You send."

"Never mind. Let me sleep."

"You suggested it."

"I've changed my mind."

"Son of a bitch. Always the same damn shit."

"I'm sending. Go on."

"Do you see it clearly?"

"Yes."

"I see a triangle."

I didn't say anything.

"A triangle, that's all. I see a triangle, Miller. What are you sending?"

"Jesus Christ. Jee-zuss Chrice. I've got chills everywhere."

"Tell me what you were sending."

"A diamond. First a sailboat with a white, triangular sail, then a diamond. I sent the diamond."

I turned. Her eyes were waiting for me.

"You and me," I whispered.

"We're the same, Miller. Aren't we?"

I kissed her on the mouth. "If you want to change your mind, say so."

"I am you," she whispered, kissing me. "Let's play more."

"I'll call Max and tell him not to come."

"He isn't coming, anyway. Let's play more."

"I'm sleepy."

"It's my turn to send."

"I'm very sleepy."

"You are a son of a bitch."

"Enough. I haven't slept for days."

"What about me? Don't you ever think about me? I warn you, Miller, don't go to sleep. I'll do something."

"I want to sleep."

"Miller, I see something. Quick. Please."

"A flower."

"You see a flower?"

"It's red."

"What kind of flower? I was sending a parachute."

"That's it, Mildred. A parachute flower."

"Fuck you, Miller."

"You, too. Let me sleep."

"Miller, I still see something. Hurry. Try again."

I lay still, eyes shut. Nothing came to me except a knock at the door, so quiet I imagined I hadn't heard it. She said, "Was that a knock?"

I sat up and listened, then got out of bed and went to the door. It was Max and Sleek. Max nodded hello. Sleek stepped backwards, but a smile moved in his pallor. I said, "Hi." I heard Mildred rushing to the kitchen sink and held them at the door. "Only one room and a kitchen," I said. Max nodded again. The smile faded slowly in Sleek's pale, flat face. Water crashed, then she was shooting to the closet, jamming into heels, scrambling a blouse on her back. A light went on. She slashed her mouth with lipstick. "Come in, come in."

They came in.

"Please sit down."

Max sat down in his coat, looked into the folds across his lap, and began to roll a cigarette. Sleek sat down in his coat, too, watching Max. Both of them glanced once at Mildred, then at each other. I said, then Max said. Sleek laughed feebly as if suppressing a cough. Then they both stared at her. Max offered her the first drag on the cigarette. She said quickly, but in a soft voice, cool, shy. They looked at one another, Max and Sleek, and agreed with their eyes: she was a smart little girl. I sat down. I told them she might be pregnant. We were thinking about getting married, I said. I was going to look for a new job. Everyone laughed at something. Max said, Sleek said. They took off their coats. She was now shining awake, feeling herself, being looked at.

"Do you want some coffee?" She tossed her hair slightly with the question.

Max said, "Do you have milk?"

Sleek said, "Coffee."

She curled tightly in her chair, legs underneath, making knees, shins, ankles to look at. They looked. I stood up and went into the kitchen for the coffee and milk. Max was saying and Sleek added. She was quick again, laughing, doing all right for herself. I took my time, then came back in with the coffee and milk. I asked what they were into lately, imports, exports, hustlers, what. Sleek sucked the cigarette. Max rolled another and was looking at Mildred. He asked if she had considered an abortion. She smiled. Sleek said I was an old friend. He would get us a discount. They wouldn't take their cut until I had a new job. They shook their heads. No cut. Max mentioned a doctor in Jersey, a chiropractor on Seventy-second Street. He said his own girl had had an abortion and died. Almost drove him nuts. He drank like a pleeb. You have to get a clean doctor. Otherwise it can be discouraging. His stable was clean. Sleek nodded shrewdly, something tight in his face, as if he knew. "Of course," he said. "Of course." He opened his hand and showed Mildred some pills. She raised an eyebrow, shrugged, looked at me. I was grinning, almost blind.

"Do what you like."

She took a pill. I took a pill, too. Max talked about the eggbeater they use and what comes out, little fingers, little feet. Mildred squirmed, showed a line of thigh, feel of hip, ankles shaped like fire.

"Abortions are safe," I said and waved a hand.

"Right," said Max. He tossed a pill into his mouth.

Sleek said he had a new kind of pill. Mildred asked shyly with her eyes. He offered immediately. She took it. "The whole country shoves pills up itself," he said. "My mother takes stoppies at night and goies in the morning." He gleamed, sucked the cigarette, and sat back as if something had been achieved.

Max frowned, mentioned his dead girl and said

it hadn't been his baby. He shook his head, grinding pity, and said, "Discouraging."

"Your mother?" asked Mildred.

Sleek said she lived in Brooklyn. I nodded as if to confirm that he had a mother. He whispered, "The womb is resilient. Always recovers." Max said, "Made of steel." "Of course," said Sleek, "chicks are tough." Mildred agreed, sat up, showed us her womb. Max took it, squeezed, passed it to Sleek. He suppressed a laugh, then glanced at me.

"Squeeze, squeeze," I said.

He said, "Tough number. Like steel."

I said it looked edible. Sleek stared at Mildred. She got up and took her womb to the stove. I had a bite. Max munched and let his eyelids fall to show his pleasure. Sleek took a sharp little bite and made a smacking noise in his mouth. I felt embarrassed, happy. Mildred seemed happy, seeing us eat. I noticed her grope furtively for something else to eat. But it was late now. Rain banged like hammers, no traffic moved in the street. They waited for a few more minutes, then Max yawned, belched, stood up. "We'll get a cab on Sixth Avenue," he said to Sleek. I said we would decide, then get in touch with him right away. We thanked them for the visit. I apologized for not being more definite. Max shrugged.

They were in the neighborhood, anyway. Sleek said take a couple of days to think about it. Gay things were said at the door. Max said, Sleek said, Mildred laughed goodbye. Their voices and feet went down the stairs.

Mildred kicked off her shoes. I turned out the light. We kissed. I put my hand between her legs. She began to cry.

"You may not love me, Miller, but you'll cry when I'm gone."

"Stop it," I said.

She cried. I made fists and pummeled my head. She cried. I pummeled until my head slipped into my neck. She stopped crying. I smashed my mouth with my knee. She smiled a little.

"Do it again."

I started eating my face. She watched, then her eyes grew lazy, lids like gulls, sailing down. She lay back and spread underneath like a parachute. I lay beside her and looked at the window. It was black and shining with rain. I said, "I like your hair, Mildred, your eyes, your nose, your legs. I love your voice." She breathed plateaus and shallow, ragged gullies. She slept on her back, mouth open, hands at her sides, turned up. Rain drilled the window. Thunder burdened the air.

Fingers and Toes

I SCRIBBLED A HASTY NOTE, REGRETFUL, TO THE
point. Fourteen pages, sharp as knives. I refuse. I
don't feel good. The date is inconvenient. Sorry.
Sorry. Sorry. Then I stopped and sat rigid as a
sphinx. Henry was my dearest friend. It was brutal
not to mitigate such severity. Not many people
count in one's life. A fool slams doors. Who knows,
given the vicissitudes, where a man has to grovel
tomorrow? I sprang forward and said as much. I
told him his company was more precious to me than
my own. I'd love to come to your dinner party, I said.
Nothing short of atomic holocaust can prevent it.
You're a man of genius and personality. You give
life to my life. But refuse, I must. To be frank,
Henry, it's impossible for me to come. You are a per-

son who doesn't like me. Why? I could say this or that, but who knows his own deficiencies? Who? We know each other too well these days, but who, who among us knows what the others know? The mystery of self lies here, Henry. There in the hearts of others. Consider how often we've laughed at a mutual friend and said, That's just like him, or, You know Ahab would do that sort of thing. Yet the man himself, Henry, does he say these things? No. He goes his way, grinning, tipping his hat, waving to friends on every side. He goes ass out in the eyes of the world. I flew to the mirror, ripped down my pants. I flew back and said, Henry, I read books, I go to the movies, I look constantly in mirrors both literal and figurative. But do I see anything? How could I? I'm not my friend. I'm not Henry. I'm Phillip, Henry. Your friend. I could say things about you that would make your nipples pucker. As for your invitation let me say I am delighted to accept it. I reread the note, chucked up laughs like the clap of big buttocks, and flushed it down the bowl. The one I sent was a stream of polite, innocuous drivel. Twenty-five pages. Pleasing to hear from him, I said. I confessed that I loved to get letters, especially invitations. For just that alone I was grateful to him. I wished so much I could come to his dinner party. Nothing I'd rather, but I had stomach cancer and had to pass it up.

Some future date perhaps when they cut out my stomach, etc., etc. I was sitting beside the phone nibbling Dexedrine when he called.

"I just read your letter, Phillip. Woo, what a letter. I'm sorry you're sick."

"My feet are like sea shells, Henry."

"No."

"Sea shells. Curled, hard, I walk bonky, bonky."

"Phillip, you're not the only one. Every time I lose touch with a friend something terrible happens to him. I could go on and on. I hate letters."

"Mine was impulsive. I'll never write you again."

"I hate to walk in the street, Phillip. I might meet some friend about to kill himself. I sneak everywhere. I wanted to talk to you, by the way, about our dinner party. And now look. I intended to say a few words to make you change your mind. This is what I get."

"Months of silence, Henry. Things happen."

"I couldn't leave well enough alone. Besides, Marjorie insisted. 'Call Phillip. Call Phillip,' she said. Such a trivial matter, one night, a dinner party. The truth is, Phillip, there aren't many people in one's life who count. I could ask seventy or eighty people for that night, but how many of them would be you?"

"I was going to kill myself that night."

"Are you saying you won't come?"

"But I'll come."

"I knew you would. I know you so well, Phillip. You have no convictions."

I laughed. He did, too. Nee, nee, nee. Behind him somewhere Marjorie clapped her mouth. Nee, nee filtered through, female, insidious. Henry snarled. I did, too. Footsteps hurried away and I knew there was going to be trouble. From a distance Marjorie screamed, "I laugh, I pee and I don't care who knows it." Henry said, "I'll call you back, Phillip." "Just tell him to come," she screamed.

I quivered all over. It was excruciating to bear such knowledge. The private life of a friend is to be dreamed about, never known. I went to the bathroom and stepped under a hot shower. Wax coiled out of my ears like snakes. The phone rang again. "Henry," I said, "didn't you call earlier?" I picked up the phone. "Henry," I said, and he said, "Then we'll expect you, Phillip."

"Of course."

"It wasn't of course a little while ago."

His voice was hard and mean. I remembered he could be that way and shook my head.

"You know me, Henry."

"Of course, of course, but I'd as soon you stayed in your rathole downtown if you don't feel like coming."

"Just tell me when."

"Next Wednesday. Six-thirty. Perhaps you can't make it at such a wild hour?"

"It's perfect. One of the best times. It gives me pleasure just to think about it."

"You ought to hang up the phone and masturbate."

"Don't be silly. I'll just open the window."

Nee, nee we laughed. I grinned and shook my head. I remembered how witty he could be.

"And another thing, Phillip. It's not crucial, but I want to say it."

"Please."

"I know about you and Marjorie, Phillip."

"Don't say it."

"Makes no difference. We're civilized people, not Victorians. What's finished is finished, no more, void. What remains is friendship. Our friendship. Even stronger than before. I hope you feel the same way. That's how Marjorie feels."

"That's how I feel, too, Henry."

"Then there isn't anything more to be said about that. Am I right?"

"You're right."

"Are you absolutely sure? I don't like to leave things unsaid, Phillip. They always come out one way or another."

"I know, I know. Henry, I get boils on my neck when I leave things unsaid."

"Good, then you understand me. Next Wednesday, Phillip. Six-thirty."

"Right."

Nee, nee we laughed and said goodbye.

Dinner with them was out. Furthermore I wouldn't eat a thing. Not that night and not until that night. The idea just came to me. I didn't struggle to establish thesis and antithesis. It came BOOMBA. Real ideas strike like eagles. A man who loves premises and conclusions loves a whore. I wouldn't eat that night and not until that night. That's how well he knew me. Not at all.

I ran about my room until I got sleepy and then spent the night whirling in bed shrieking curses. At dawn I was sitting up with two fists of hair, cool as a buddha. Dinner with them was out. The idea gave me shivers. Fat ran off. Bones lifted under the skin. I went and leaned against the refrigerator door. Hours passed, the day, the night. I leaned with the insouciance of a hoodlum or a whore. I gazed down at my feet. Gaunt, sharp as chicken feet. The objective principles on which I stood. The first line of a poem came to me: "Bitter, proud metatarsals." I smelled chicken salad and cream cheese, but didn't move until I ripped open the refrigerator door, grabbed handfuls of salad and cheese and flung them out the window. "Ya, ya," I shouted, "food is out." My hand seized a frozen steak and flung it into my mouth. I swallowed. Instantly, I became depressed. The steak was in. Like a virgin deflowering I sank to the floor. The steak worked grimly inside. I wanted to make it stop. My stomach churned like the back of a garbage truck. Arteries sucked. I had the steak in my neck, thighs, fingers, toes. But all right, I thought. I'll journey to the end of the night like St. Augustine and the Marquis de Sade. The more things are different the more they are the same. Immoral is moral.

I went to the nearest restaurant, a fish house. It made no difference. I ate a cow, I'd eat a fish. I ordered lobster Leningrad and a plate of mixed crawlers, flung everything inside and chewed in a deliberate way. In my mind I said, "Yum." The waiter refilled my bread basket. I grunted, "Thanks." People like me, he said, made his job meaningful. I told him I understood food. He nodded.

"May I watch?"

"Please," I said.

He stood beside my chair and put his hand discreetly on my shoulder. His mouth moved with mine. When I finished he smiled and asked if I enjoyed the meal. I rubbed my stomach and winked. He nodded in an appreciative way. I leaped from my chair. We embraced. "My name is Phillip," I said. He said he could tell. I squeezed money into his hand. He protested. I refused to listen, squeezed more, snapped up the menu and shoved it down into my crotch.

Days passed. The dinner party was only hours away. As it drew closer I couldn't repress what Henry had said. He knew I was going to come. He knew me so well. "But you were very wrong," I said. However wrong I could indulge the idea that he was right. I indulged it: "You were right." The idea gave me pleasure. The pleasure of an infant. Something turned, poked, smelled, very known. I bobbled out into the street and walked among strangers to intensify the pleasure. None of them knew me. I went to a liquor store and bought wine, red and white, to express my contempt for Henry's dinner. A bottle of Armenian khaki was on sale. I bought it too, then left and bought flowers. Around midnight I stood outside Henry's door. It was open, welcoming the night. There were seventy or eighty people in the house. I knocked. Henry came running. "Someone's at the door," he yelled. "Phillip. What a surprise."

I leaped backward into the darkness. He leaped after me and caught my arm. "Come in, come in." He took my wine and flowers and flung them into a closet. "We had a little dinner party."

"I already had dinner. Thanks for inviting me in, Henry. I can't stay."

"Why not?"

"I'd rather not talk about it. It's nothing personal."

"But Phillip, I want to talk to you."

"Let me continue for a moment. Then I'm going back to my rathole. I appreciate your invitation more than I can tell you. You believe me?"

"Of course."

"Don't say of course. I really mean it."

"I do too, of course."

"Don't say of course, Henry. You mean a great deal to me. You're my dearest friend, the only one I have. It kills me not to come to your dinner party. But I can't. Let's not talk about it, all right? I don't ask a lot of favors of you."

"Will you have a drink?"

"Bourbon."

"Ice? Water?"

"No. In fact, look, don't even pour it into the glass."

I snapped up the bottle and swallowed. People were everywhere, standing, sitting, talking, smoking, drinking. It was a brilliant crowd. The women had nice legs. The men looked as if it didn't matter. I felt a bit out of place because I didn't know any of them. Henry touched my elbow. He spoke very quietly, very slowly, and as if we were the only ones there.

"Phillip, I do want to talk to you."

I was thrilled by the intensity of his voice.

"There's nothing to talk about at a party," I said.

He shrugged. "You're right, Phillip."

"What do you want to talk about?"

He shrugged again. It was very like him to do that when he had a lot on his mind. "About? You're hungry for topics? I want more than to talk about. I want dialogue, Phillip, not topics. I don't want to talk about a thing. Things crap up talk."

"I agree. Now I'm going, Henry."

"Go."

"But I'll listen for a minute if you like."

"Can you listen for a minute? Don't say yes if you can't."

"I'll listen for a minute."

"Phillip, I'm going out of my mind."

"Why?"

"I couldn't tell you in a million years."

"It's been good talking to you, Henry."

"Wait, Phillip. I want to tell you a story. Not a story, a parable."

"Oh."

"It represents my connection with the elemental life. Nothing else. Not art, not politics, not history, not anything but the elemental life. The truth is, Phillip, I don't give a damn about anything else. I'm talking about love."

"I know. I can tell."

"Of course. Phillip, listen. The first time Marjorie and I went out we went to a movie. I don't remember what was playing. At any rate I put my arm around her and my hand fell on her breast. She didn't say anything. She trembled. At first, Phillip, I didn't notice where my hand had fallen. Then I felt her trembling and I noticed. I trembled. I was a hand. She was a breast. I don't have to tell you what a trembling breast feels like."

"Don't tell me."

"I've gone too far now to stop."

"No more about the breast."

"If I stop I'll be like Satan floating in space or Macbeth on his way to stab Duncan. Imagine if they had stopped. They would have felt like creeps. It's the kind of thing, Phillip, you have to get over with."

"Get it over with. You trembled, she trembled."

"I was a hand. She was a breast. One day, not much later, I touched her you know where and said, 'You tremble.' I told her I noticed and wondered if she noticed. More than that I wondered if she noticed that I noticed. Never in my life was I so sincerely concerned about anything. It was a feeling. Do you follow me, Phillip? I knew immediately it was a feeling. Clear, authentic, like you standing here this minute. You're standing here, right? Nothing less. That's how this was. Nothing less."

"I see. What happened?"

"Phillip, I could spring up on her like an Irish setter and she wouldn't notice unless I called it to her attention."

"I don't know what to say."

"Say what you think. Say whatever you think."

"You lost your connection with the elemental life, is that it?"

"You could say that."

"At least you have dialogue, Henry. Where's Marjorie, by the way? I don't see her anywhere."

"Do you see that door? Go through it, you'll find her."

I looked at the door. It had a quality of shutness. I looked at Henry's face. It had the same quality, something vertical and shut, like the face of a mountain. Impassive, forbidding, beckoning, irresistible. Susceptibilities in my hands and feet became agitated.

"I won't go through any doors, Henry."

"I wouldn't have talked about this with anyone but you, Phillip."

"I'm flattered, but not another word, please."

"In that room, Phillip, in the dark, in a corner . . ."

"I'm leaving now."

I glanced away. He glanced after me. He arrived, I was gone. I turned back and looked him directly around the eyes, a swimming look. He tried to pierce it but wallowed. His eyes flailed for a grip but I widened my focus. "Phillip," he cried, "go speak to her. Tell her my love."

"Ech," I said. "I knew it would come to this. Tell her yourself. I'm going."

"Go. You have no right to go, but go. I've told you everything. Take it. Throw it in a sewer someplace."

"Be reasonable. What can I say to her?"

"Don't play stupid. You and she had plenty to say to each other before I came along. Say anything, just make her come out or let me come in."

"Henry."

"You owe me this. I'll never feel it's over between you unless you do it. Make her call me in there."

"What if I can't?"

"Then I'll know what it means and I'll kill you.

To me the connection between love and death is very close."

"Henry."

His hand clutched my elbow like the claw of an angry bird. He walked me to the door.

"Henry, what can I do?"

"You know what."

He opened the door and shoved me through it. The door shut and I was in such darkness that I staggered and swayed. The sound of clinking glasses and talking trickled in after me, but I felt no relation to it. I was steeped, immobilized, wrapped up tight as a mummy. I was without head or arms or feet and my brain was suspended like a cloud. "Marjorie," I said. My voice whooshed away. No answer came. I crooned, "Marjorie, it's Phillip." A hiss cut the dark and there was a rough scratching like scales on rocks. "Marjorie," I crooned again, bending slowly until my hands touched the floor. "It's Phillip. I know you're there." I was on my hands and knees, whispering, urgent and conspiratorial. I leaned forward and put out my hand, letting it drift into the blackness like a little boat. I heard breathing. My hand drifted into it. My eyes bulged. I leaned after my hand, saw nothing, but smelled her very close and felt her heat on my face. The hiss came again. My hand drifted further into the darkness, my fingertips quivering,

quickening to the shape, the texture, the person of
Marjorie. There was a slash. My hand snapped back.

"Don't try that again, jackass," she said.

"My hand is bleeding."

"Good."

"Henry has a lot of friends out there, Marjorie.
Why don't you step outside for a moment and slash
them up?"

"Give me your hand."

"Fat chance."

"Give it to me. I didn't mean to hurt you."

My hand drifted forward. She took it in both of
hers and licked it.

"Better?"

"Feels all right."

I started to draw my hand back again. She
hissed, clutched it tightly. I dragged. She wrapped
herself around it, shimmied up my arm and hung
from my shoulder like a bunch of bananas. She
whimpered in my ear, "Phillip, I'm miserable."

I patted her knee with my free hand. She tightened her grip with her legs and pressed her face into
my neck.

"It's not me they'll meet if I go out there. Not the
me I am."

I felt sexual irritation and started patting her
harder.

"I know what you mean."

"Phillip, when I woke up this morning there was something lying right beside me. You know what?"

"What?" I said, patting, patting. "Henry?"

"Me. Stretched out right beside me and staring at me in such a sad way."

"It's the *Zeitgeist,* Marjorie."

Blood stopped flowing in my arm. I tried to move it. She squeezed.

"Me," she said. "I want me, me, me."

I tried to shrug her off but it was like trying to shrug off a big wart. I smeared her against the floor, got up and smeared her against a wall. She clung like my head on my neck, my foot on my leg. I rolled, rammed into tables and chairs. She clung. I leaped up and came down on her. She clung. She gnawed my neck, nibbled, licked, squeezed. I stopped and lay still. I tried to think, but darkness seeped into my ideas, clogged the parts and connections with heavy, impenetrable scum. Her fingers and toes worked into me like worms, coiling around tendons and bones. I could tell she was nervous and said, "Marjorie, as long as I'm here why don't you tell me what's wrong. I'll listen. Something wrong between you and Henry, for example?"

"There's nothing wrong."

"Is it this party? Don't you like this party?"

"I love it."

"But there is something wrong?"

"Nothing."

Instinctively, I wanted to punch her in the head. I said, "Marjorie, for all I care you can fester in here. Let me go."

She licked and squeezed.

"If you don't let go I'll punch you in the head."

She plunged her tongue into my ear. I breathed hard. Glaciers streamed down my face. Suddenly we heard footsteps approach the door and both of us lay still.

"You ask me what's modern," said a man. "No one feels anymore. That's modern."

Earrings tinkled as if a head were being shaken violently. A necklace rattled. "But I feel you can't say that," cried a girl. "I feel there are a lot of feelings today, feelings we feel deeply and that's why it feels as if we don't. I couldn't dance otherwise. How could I dance if I didn't? Answer that."

For a moment there was silence. Then the man spoke again, his voice dismal and pinched as if he had a finger in one nostril.

"Feel shmeel."

Marjorie whispered, "You feel, don't you?"

"I feel," I said, "but this is life. Who feels?" I thrashed. She clutched and bit. I collapsed and lay still. There was a bump against the door, hard rubbing, then a kick.

"Don't touch me," said a girl. "Look what you did to my dress. I think you suffer from jugular peacocks."

Others came by, stopped.

"Miss Genitalia, I'd like you to meet Miss Gapegunda."

"I'm sure she'll come back, Max. It's not like her to run out. She doesn't have carfare."

"If she comes back I'll spit in her face."

Marjorie was breathing as if she were asleep. I listened to her and to the people who came by and stopped outside the door.

"What you said, Irma, makes a lot of sense," said a man.

"I was just talking."

"But very intelligently."

"You can't mean that. I was talking, that's all. If you don't talk at these parties they think you're a fool."

"I do mean it. I'd like you to write it all up and submit it to my journal. Do you write German?"

Another man wheezed.

"Shut up, sweetheart. All right? Just once you shut up, all right? It's not so much to ask, is it? I say yes, you say no. I say no, you say yes. Why don't you write a book and shut up? Write one of mine in reverse. Where I say no you say yes."

"Fuck you, Ned."

Marjorie was asleep, wrapped around my arm like ten snakes. I moved a little. She constricted and said, "Nya, nya."

I lay still again and gaped into the darkness. It was important to think. I had a sense of the problematic towering above me in the darkness like a Gothic cathedral. Complex, violent, full of contradictions like the hairdo of a madwoman. I fell asleep. In my sleep I heard a knock at the door. It came drifting over waters like Noah's dove, little grey wings knocking through fog. It came closer, closer. I cried, "Here, little dovey." It went by, knocking dimly away into the fog.

"Phillip," said Henry.

I yelled in my dream, "Henureee."

Marjorie woke up, hissed, "Don't answer."

I tried to wake up.

"Phillip, you there? Who's there?"

Marjorie began moving all over me. She ripped open my shirt. She scraped off my shoes with her toes. I woke up as my zipper went down like a slashed throat. She wrenched under me. I said,

"Love." She yelled and pummeled my back as if sending messages to friends across the veldt. "What's wrong?" I said.

"I like it, I like it," she yelled.

"Like what?" I said.

"Who's in there?" said Henry.

"Don't come in," I said.

His footsteps went away.

Marjorie went limp, her arms outflopped, languid as lily stalks.

"Finish," she said.

Her legs fell apart as if cleaved by an axe.

"Hurry," she said.

I hurried. Footsteps came back to the door. There was a knock.

"Marjorie," said Henry. "Was that you in there?" I hurried.

"Wait for me," she said. "Slow down."

"Of course," said Henry. "You know I will." I slowed down.

"Do it," she said.

"I won't move an inchy winchy until you tell me to." He made a kissing against the door.

"Up and down, up and down," she said.

"Ha, ha," said Henry. He jumped up and down, up and down. "Like this?"

"Yeah, yeah."

Nee, nee, nee he laughed. "Here I go up and down, up and down," he sang. "I'm skipping rope."

"Now," she yelled.

"Now?" said Henry. "Di oo say now now?"

"Wow, wow," she said.

"Marjorie," I said.

"Henry," she screamed.

He flung open the door. I was behind it. He laughed nee, nee, jumped up and down and came skipping into the room. I flew out. His knees struck the floor like cannon balls.

"Marjorie," he said.

"Love."

I got my flowers and wine and slipped out into the night. It was moonless and cold. I slipped into it nose first. It nosed into me. I twitched like a fish and went quivering through dingy dingles, from blackness to blackness to blackness to blackness.

Isaac

TALMUDIC SCHOLAR, MASTER OF CABALA, ISAAC
felt vulnerable to a thousand misfortunes in New
York, slipped on an icy street, lay on his back and
wouldn't reach for his hat. People walked, traffic
screamed, freezing damp sucked through his clothes.
He let his eyes fall shut—no hat, no freezing, no
slip, no street, no New York, no Isaac—and got a
knock against the soles of his shoes. It shook his
teeth. His eyes flashed open, darkness spread above
him like a predatory tree, a dozen buttons glared
and a sentence flew out, beak and claws, with a
quality of moral sophistication indistinguishable
from hatred: "What's-a-matta, fuckhead, too much
vino?" He'd never heard of vino, but had a feeling
for syntax—fuckhead was himself. He said, "Eat pig

shit," the cop detected language, me-it became I-thou and the air between them a warm, viable medium. He risked English: "I falled on dot ice, tenk you."

The man in the next bed wasn't alive. Gray as a stone, hanging over the edge of the mattress, the head was grim to consider. But only a fool points out the obvious; Isaac wouldn't tell a nurse. Even so, he couldn't dismiss a head upside down, staring at him, and found himself crying. He had traveled thousands of miles to fall down like a fuckhead and lay beside a corpse. Crying loosened muscles. His shoulders began moving. Shoulders moving, he discovered arms moving, and if arms, why not legs? In his left leg moved thunder and lightning. But he sat up and shouted, "Sitting!" A nurse ripped open his pajamas and shoved in a bedpan. "I appreciate," he said, and defecated.

Before dawn he had dressed himself and was in the street. Stumbling, pressing into the dark as if pursued by dogs. More and more he tilted left and thus, beneath horrible pain, felt horrible geometry. His left leg was shorter than his right. He pressed into a phone booth. His sister screamed when she heard his voice. He told her what happened and she screamed, "Don't move." He sat in the booth, fell asleep, there was a knock and his eyes opened. She looked through the glass. "Katya," he said, "like a coffin." She wouldn't discuss the idea. Neither would Chaim, her husband, or Fagel, her husband's sister, or hunchback Yankel, the peddler, who asked where Isaac felt pain. In the back? In the leg? He remembered a fall in which he hurt his knee. Did Isaac's knee hurt? No? Very strange. How did a scholar, he wondered, fall in the street like an animal; but then what's one leg shorter compared to a brain concussion with blood bulging from the eyes? No comparison. Lucky Isaac. Isaac winked, made a little lucky nod, and collapsed. Fagel screamed. Katya screamed. Chaim gave Isaac his umbrella. Isaac pressed it with one hand. The other pressed his sister's arm. They went down the street together—Isaac, Katya, Fagel, Chaim, Yankel. Cracow, the chiropractor, had an office nearby.

To keep his mind off his stumbling torture, Katya told Isaac about Moisse, who wasn't lucky. He came to New York sponsored by a diamond merchant, friend of politicians, bon vivant, famous for witty exegeses of the Talmud. "So?" So as a condition of sponsorship, Moisse promised never to abandon, in New York, any tradition of the faith. He imagined no circumstances in which he might, but married, opened a dry-goods store, and had a son. Circumstances arose in doctor bills. He had to do business on Saturdays. Isaac licked his lips. Chaim punched his chest. Yankel shrugged his hunch. "So?" So it followed like the manifestation in the garden, that the merchant's beard hung in the door one Saturday. —You know what day this is, Moisse? What could he say? Isaac said, "Nothing. What could he say?" Chaim punched, Yankel shrugged. The beard nodded. The mouth hacked up a spittle, the spittle smacked the floor, and the baby son was discovered on the prostrate body of his mother, shrieking like a demon while he ate the second nipple. Now Moisse doesn't do business on Saturday. His worst enemies won't say he isn't a saint.

"You got another story?"

"It's the only story I know."

"Tell me again," said Isaac.

Before she finished they were inside an old brownstone, looking up a high, narrow stairway. She tugged at the umbrella, but Isaac only looked, as if they were stairs in a dream. To be looked at, nothing else. What can you do in a dream? She tugged. He fell against a wall. She went up alone and came down with, "Doctor Cracow says." Isaac must walk up and lay face down on the chiropractor table. Otherwise go away and shrivel. In a week his leg would be a raisin. He could look forward to carrying it in his armpit. Fagel screamed, Chaim punched. They walked up.

Cracow stood suddenly erect, as if, the instant before, he had touched his toes. His fingers were stiff, quivering like the prongs of a rake. He nodded to the table. Isaac dropped onto it as if into an abyss and Cracow pummeled him from neck to tail, humming: "*Muss es sein. Es muss sein*," then said, "Get up." With dreamlike speed they were at the brink of the stairs. A thing whooshed by, cracked, clattered to the landing. "Get it," said Cracow.

Isaac shook his head.

"Isaac, get it," said Katya. Chaim said, "Get it." Yankel said, "Get it, get it."

The umbrella was a streak of wood and cloth in another world. Isaac shook his head at the possibility of getting it. Beyond that, not getting it. Shaking his head, he started down. Not with delicate caution, like a man just crippled, but mechanical exactitude, like a man long crippled. Even in the bones of former incarnations, crippled, resigned to a thousand strictures. Cracow hummed, Isaac descended. Every step an accident succeeding an accident in a realm where perfection was grotesque. Cracow said, "No pain?"

Isaac stopped, gazed out; then, carefully, into his own center. Pain? His whole being was a question. It trembled toward yes or no and, like music, yes, very slightly, yes, he felt himself lift and fly above the stairs. Then he settled like dust. Cracow's voice shot through the air: "Six dollars, please." Isaac turned to fly up to him. With four wings clapping he was struck by stairs, smacked by walls, stopped by the ultimate, unyielding floor. He lay on his back. His eyes fell shut. Thumps accumulated down the stairs. Katya screamed. Yankel shrugged, Chaim whispered, "Dead?" Fagel screamed, Cracow said, "Could be dead." Chaim said, "Dead?" Fagel screamed, Katya screamed. "Dead? Dead?" said Yankel. Chaim said, "Not alive," and Yankel said, "Dead." Fagel screamed, screamed, screamed, screamed, screamed.

A Green Thought

I YELLED; SHE RAN IN; I POINTED. "WHY IS IT green?" She clapped her mouth; I shrieked, "Why is it green?" She answered . . . I shrieked, "Vatchinol infection!" She whispered . . . "Green medicine!" I wouldn't let her mitigate; shoved her aside. "No mitigations!" She picked up a washcloth. I wouldn't let her wash it. "No washing it!" I lunged into my clothes, laughed ironically, slammed out . . . Subway steps, downtown express, eighty miles an hour. Hot, cold, nauseated. Nevertheless, nevertheless, nevertheless. Not like the last time, fighting, fighting, collapse: leetlekissywissysuckyfucky. I checked my fly. Light tight. But I sensed the green, looked away. No one noticed. Good fly. Develop photos inside. A lady sucked her teeth. Suck. Suck.

The man beside me did a crossword puzzle, picked his nose. Suck. Pick. Everyone busy. New Yorkers in the raging underground. Sensuous. Insular. Discreet. All buried in noise. I vomited. Quick. No one noticed. Used my shoe; slipped foot back in; looked up cooly at the ads: have a lot of fun; worry about communism; smoke; drink. They made a sense of community. Lot of fun all around. The lady sucked her teeth, the man did his puzzle, picked his nose. Train full of pleasure. Involvement. I liked the mood. I philosophized: what does this mean to ride downtown? eighty miles an hour? three o'clock in the morning? shoe full of vomit? I noticed a girl leaning against her date. A marine. She had frog eyes; motionless, dreaming of flies. Looked something like a moron. It all meant nothing. I had slammed, certain it meant something. I'd laughed ironically. She opened the door. I waited ironically for the elevator. I felt her stare, grey, foggy, rotten with guilt. She said, "Your face, Phillip." I whirled. "Gimme carfare." A flash of white ass, of blonde. She vanished, returned, wrist-deep-crap clicking in her purse. She struggled, naked, shameless. I was cool. She pulled out a dollar. Green. I was sick, getting sicker. Rocking, banging, rocking, banging. But this was the last time. I sang it to the mambo of the wheels: "The last time, the last time. Chunga cha-

chunga. Green green." I'd soon have to walk. Deserted buildings, warehouses, alleys, cats, rats,
drunks, unpredictable figments of the municipal
dark. City at night, full of wonders, mysteries. Like
a god. I could hardly wait to get home, lock the
door, lie down, sleep. But I might run into neighborhood kids, get robbed, chopped up, set on fire,
pissed on, stuck in a garbage can. That would mean
the city hated me. I appreciated its hatred, shared
it, wanted to fling out to the speeding tunnel. But
I looked at the marine and his girl: both pale, tight
in the face, yet healthy. I'd seen him before. On
toilet walls. Her, too, waiting for him, cock and
balls. It might have been us: Mr. and Miss Subway.
No such luck. Cecily had a high I Q, degree from
Barnard. I giggled a lot. The moron leaned on the
marine. I looked for a moral. They swayed against
the rocking iron tumultuous rush as . . . they
would sway against the buffets of life. I was envi-
ous; felt ashamed: my insularity, my self-pitying.
I wanted to shove them off the train. I wanted to go
back, pound on her door. She would open it. I'd
giggle. But I knew the rules. It was her move. Love
is not enough. Hell with her. Blond hair, grey eyes,
white skin, green crotch. Every conceivable virtue.
Happens to be festering in the vagina. Take good
with bad. I giggled ironically. The man covered his

puzzle. Inched away, erasing. Made me self-conscious, creepy feeling. I wanted to strangle him. I
yelled, "No one can solve the puzzle!" He gave me
a look as if that hadn't occurred to him before. I
shrugged. He changed his seat. I sprawled like a
vulgar swine, yawned, scratched my ass, studied
the marine and his girl, objects, paragons. My
mother used to say, "Why don't you be like Ken-
neth? . . . like Bernard? . . . like Schmuckhead?
Why don't you do the right thing, Phillip?" Why
don't I be like that marine? No sideburns to catch
filth, unbalance his head. Just a haze of needles
prickling at the top. And her hair: thick, red, bulging around her ears like meat. Such radical difference: Mr. Prickles and Miss Meat. What could their
relationship consist in? "None of that rooting in my
horn, Marie. Try it, I'll kick your twot off." She
melts. He upchucks like a tilted jug. Take that, that.
Spilling marines. Moral. But I was moral, too. I had
slammed out. Exquisite dinner, wines, dessert in
bed. Naked, satisfied, peeing hard into the roaring
center and the whole toilet echoing to a tinkling
consonant with the force that through the green
fuse drives beyond right things, wrong things, and
"CECILY," I yelled, the train retching passed Bloom-
ingdale's. She did it on purpose. The train stopped.

A GREEN THOUGHT

A man entered carrying a newspaper. PLANE CRASH. Green crotch strikes again. I didn't read another word. It all just came to me: fifteen hundred returning from a soccer game, team, coaches, cheering squad. Usual bunch. People shake their heads, tsk, tsk, but oneself isn't dead. Ten cents to find out one isn't dead. Cost me nothing, a glance, a second of subway lucubration. I was alive, aware of it, more than alive. I wanted to do kneebends, pushups, jog a couple of laps. Maybe the marine would join me. "Hey, schmuck, how about a little P.T. before the next stop?" He would really grin. So would his moron. But it was the next stop. Mine. I was up, striding out, step, splash, step, splash, hut-hut! I was alone. Now I could think. I shut my eyes, squeezed. I thought: "Think!" I couldn't think. It proved I was social. No lonely thinker, no Thoreau this Phillip. Which way to the pond? Let me see; I remember that pile of bird shit from yesterday. Take years just to get from shack to pond. "Simplify," said Thoreau. Really see what life is about. Indeed, just come back, that's all: here's old Phillip, schmutz and fleas; no book; maybe a little map. "See, X is the shack. Dig? The circle is the pond." What do you mean open the door, fall into the pond? I was nervous. I needed another voice. All right.

"Say something." What? "Say an important, sober, meaningful phrase." I said, "Ludwig Wittgenstein," snapped double, rolled, screeched, "What a dingleberry," rolled into a phone booth. Numbers scratched into the walls. Names. Recommendations. The city was social; how could I ever live anywhere else? "Call Carla for a first-rate toe job." I wiggled my toes. Seemed all right. I memorized her number, left the booth, ran. What I expected: deserted buildings, alleys, cats. My apartment. I had to phone someone. Green crotch was out. I grabbed the phone, dialed Henry. It was very late, but he was my friend. Marjorie answered: "Your name first, wise ass."

"Marjorie, this is Phillip. Tell Henry I'm sick."

"O.K."

She hung up.

I sat on the bed, chuckling. How silly of her to have done that. Now she had the rest of her life to wonder about what form my revenge would take. I chuckled, "Kill, kill, kill." The phone rang. I grabbed it. Henry's voice said, "Phillip? Phillip?"

"Phillip. Phillip."

"Don't tell me you're sick."

"Of course not."

I cracked the receiver against the wall, let it crash to the floor.

He piped: "Pheeleep, Pheeleep . . . Sometheen hapeen tee Pheeleep, Marjoreep."

I pushed over a chest of drawers.

"Pheeeep, Pheeeep."

I sang, "La, la," and vomited on the receiver.

"Pheeweep wa dee mawee? . . . dee oo ha fie wee Ceceeweep?"

I felt better, hung up, undressed. I lay down, shut my eyes, began screwing Ceceeweep, but everyone was jumping, shouting, except the marine and me. There had been a crash. He nodded in my direction. I nodded back, very pleased to have been recognized by a person like him, with his moral haircut. The man dropped his crossword puzzle, yelled, "Breakdown. There's been a serious breakdown." He started to masturbate, but the train wouldn't move and suddenly, pop, he ripped his prick off. I screamed and a girl said, "Phillip, what's wrong?"

"Who?"

"A succubus."

I tried to smile. "You come back later, baby. I'm a tad indisposed."

She stood beside the bed, didn't move. I heard her breathing.

"Don't stand in the vomit, sweets."

"Shit!"

"You stood in it, eh?"

"Never mind. I see you're wearing a shoe, Phillip. Do you always sleep with a shoe?"

"Get up to leak, hop right to the bowl. Saves fuss."

"Phillip, don't you want to look at me?"

"I'm sick."

"A man is the sum of his actions."

"I didn't do anything."

"I believe you, Phillip, though some would say I'm mad."

"You good succubus, baby."

"Open your eyes. I'll take my clothes off, too."

"It's cold."

A coat and trousers dropped on me. A hat, shirts, ties, laundry bag, suitcase, something heavy. I smelled it.

"Good idea."

"Do you have another rug?"

"That's the only rug."

"May I get under it with you?"

"Gimme a cigarette."

I tried to sit, but there was too much weight on my chest. She put a cigarette against my lips. I dragged.

"Light it."

"Sorry."

"Light it."

"The answer is nopey nopey."

"Get under."

I smoked. She put a leg across mine, a hand on my belly. She said, "I want to ask you something."

"Ask."

"When a man is as sick as you, inhibitions vanish, right? He'll say anything, right?"

Her lips were in my ear.

"Ask, ask."

"What do you think . . . I can't. See that. Ha, ha. I'll never get another chance like this."

"Oh, Cecily, ask, ask."

I crushed the cigarette against the wall.

"I want to ask what you think of me. What do you think of me, Phillip?"

She seized my prick.

"I like your style," I screamed.

"What else?"

"There's nothing else."

She flung my prick down.

"I didn't have to come here, Phillip. I didn't have to chase out screaming for a taxi. You talk to me, you. I asked a question. What do you think of me, Phillip?"

"There's general agreement."

"That so?"

"Pretty general fucking agreement."

"What, what do people say?"

"They say you're an asshole."

"Is that what *you* feel? Is that what *you're* telling me?"

"I'm too sick to make qualifications."

"Goodbye, Phillip. This is the last time."

I grabbed her wrist. Things hit the floor. The rug scratched everywhere. She twisted, kicked, thrashed.

"Bastard. Take a shower. You wanted to infect me."

"No one else."

"You don't love me. Say it. I want to hear you say it."

"No one else."

"You swear?"

She kissed me. I pushed down on her head.

"I'm tired, Phillip."

I pushed, pushed.

"Say you love me, Phillip."

I pushed, pushed.

"Merm," she said.

"No teeth," I yelled. "Watch the teeth."

"Mumumu."

"All right," I said.

I felt all right. All right.

Finn

Finn, lately Fein, ran into Slotsky and mentioned the change.

"By the way?"

"I agree. It goes without saying. Changing one's name isn't by the way. Neither are the harsh realities. The business world. You know what I mean, Slotsky? I was a little cavalier in my announcement. Nevertheless . . ."

"Call me Slot."

A smile wormed in Finn's lips. "That's very amusing, Snotsky."

To show Finn his smile, a smile wormed in Slotsky's lips. Reinforced by his speedy, ugly face, it was particularly revolting. But Finn, thumb hooked to alligator belt, stood six two, two hundred fifteen pounds. Imperturbable. Besides, against the big sharkskin curve of his can, he had a letter admitting him to graduate school in business administration. He also had a date that evening with Millicent Coyle at the Kappa house; darkish girl, but in manner and sisterhood fished out of the right gene pool. Black Slotsky, now, was chancy matter in the street; dog flop. Brilliant student, but pale, skinny, cross-eyed, irascible, contentious, a walking criticism of life, and a left-wing communist. In every way he seemed to beg for death. One felt his begging; also his contempt for one's reluctance to kill him on the spot. He sneered, "I thought your old name was fine."

Finn repeated, "That's very amusing, Snotsky."

"I'm still doing business under the same name."

Finn answered gently, sailing toward the Kappa house and business administration. "Granted, Slotsky. Your name is Slotsky. Mine is Finn. All right?" And he made concessions in a shrug. Two shrugs.

"Didn't it used to be Flynn?"

Finn waved bye-bye.

"Flynn, Finley . . . didn't you used to be Flanagan the rabbi?"

Finn was three, four, five steps into the evening, the life. Just up ahead there, Finn beckoned. To him, Finn.

"So long, Ferguson."

He tossed harbingers of love on his bed—
trousers, shirt, tie, socks—but couldn't decide on a
jacket to wear that evening. He wandered naked in
his indecision, lit a cigar, then considered less the
jacket than his indecision. Immediately, he discovered Slotsky in it, shimmering like fumes. Two years
ago they had been roommates. People used to say,
"You room with Slotsky?" Because Slotsky was famous. He wrote a column in the school paper, noticing films, plays, any little change in the campus ambience—Muzak in the administration building, yellow plastic chairs in the library, new pompoms
adopted by the basketball cheering squad. He was
famous for screaming revulsion and his column's
title, "Foaming at the Mouth," was a description of
himself in the throes of a criticism. Otherwise he
restricted his humor to sneering irony, never directed
at himself, never humorous. Finn explained him to
the world by saying, "He wants love. Anyhow, he
has brain cancer." It would have been easy to be
more cruel, but Slotsky helped him with chemistry
and French—Finn's reason for rooming with him
in the first place. Finn never said anything more
about Slotsky. Anything more might have suggested
there was more than an apartment between them.

There was. It started one night before end terms. Finn heard himself pleading: "I read the books, Slotsky. I took notes in class. But I can't write it. I tried all week, but I've got nothing to say about the New Deal. Do I think it was good? Bad? I think I hate poly sci, that's all. It isn't fair not to be able to drop a course in the last week. Sometimes you can't tell until the last week that you want to drop it. What am I going to do? I need the B.A. I don't want to fail. My average won't support a failure in poly sci. I'll be thrown out of here. That'll be the end of everything for Bruce J. Fein. Everything."

"What a pity."

"I'm sorry I told you about it."

"You make me a little sick, Fein."

"I make myself sick. I can't stand the sound of my voice. I'm disgusting."

He went to the bathroom, stuck three fingers into his mouth, vomited, then slept all night in his clothes. Came morning, he opened eyes full of prayer. For what, he didn't ask himself. He dragged to the kitchen, sat down at the table. It was the first time since they had been living together Slotsky hadn't gotten up ahead of him to make breakfast. Finn looked toward the next room where Slotsky slept, then looked at his hand. It lay on a pile of paper. Eighteen pages, in fact: stapled, nicely typed with double spaces, wide margins, signed Bruce J. Fein under the title, "The New Deal: Good and Bad." How could he not have felt contempt? In the next room Slotsky snored with miserable exhaustion, like a man scratching at the sides of his grave. He felt contempt bloom into hatred, bloat, blur into pity, and then, on his way to poly sci, he gradually felt something different, something new, in regard to Slotsky. He stopped for coffee. While reading through the paper, he coiled inward to catch it. He caught it in a word: he and Slotsky had "relationship." As for the paper, not bad. Not bad at all. Worth a B, maybe B+. He scratched out one phrase and scrawled his own above it. However brilliant, it was true, after all, Slotsky had never taken a course in poly sci. The correction made Finn feel as if the paper were a little bit his own. Two days later it was returned with an A++. Beneath the grade the professor had written: "Please, Fein, become a political science major, as a favor to the world." Beside his correction, Finn saw: "I will accept this because of the rest of the paper, but it is badly expressed and adds nothing to your argument." In a daze of gratitude so thrilling it reminded him of fear, Finn rushed back to the apartment, pulled a jacket out of his closet and hung rd

it in Slotsky's. Thus, among dull, shapeless gabardines, glowed a smoky tweed, a sensuous texture, a weight of life. Simply to have said, "Thank you, Slotsky, for saving my life," seemed impossible. Not that it wasn't sufficient return, but he couldn't say those words to Slotsky. Some element in their relationship would become too obvious, even grotesquely sentimental. Nevertheless, relationship, reciprocity: Finn was big, rich, good-looking and he had girls; Slotsky, in relation and return, was his roommate—he wasn't living alone with himself and the walls; Finn had the paper; Slotsky, the jacket; Finn, Slotsky; Slotsky, Finn.

On his one date that year Slotsky wore the jacket. He also wore it at a president's tea for honor students, and at an address before a learned society, he appeared in the jacket. Big on him, but, if one knew nothing else about Slotsky, one knew he owned a fine jacket. Finer than anything else he owned. One knew that because he wore it with creaseless, flapping trousers that piled at the cuffs over patent-leather, busboy shoes. He didn't seem to think the owner of such a jacket might want to wear it with trousers a bit snappier. But Finn knew Slotsky wore no jacket at all. Only an idea of a jacket—Finn's jacket—beautiful in the eyes of mankind, spilling a

superflux of beauty over anything Slotsky wore with
it, even those trousers and shoes. Over Slotsky himself, wallowing in it. Finn was gratified. The paper,
the jacket, the vision of Slotsky standing and walking
in it—reciprocity, relationship. Until this moment.

Naked before the open door of his closet, where
a harem of fifteen jackets languished—mute, lovely
receptacles of his arms and torso—Finn was struck
by the powerful idea: HIS. Then the powerful corol-
lary: he hadn't given any jacket to Slotsky forever.
When they split up he should have taken that jacket
back, but he had thought Slotsky was already too
disturbed by the loss of his roommate. He had been
very foolish: no jacket in his closet had the drape,
cut at the wrist, lapel, and haunch, or texture, tone,
and quality of material that that particular jacket
had. The one he loaned to Slotsky. Half an hour later,
sitting on the bed in Slotsky's one room, in an odor
of socks, underwear, and Slotsky, Finn had the feeling his seat would stick to the army blanket when he
stood up. Slotsky said for the third time, "You want
one of my jackets? Help yourself, roomie. I've got a
dozen classy numbers."

"*My* jacket, Slotsky."

"Take a jacket."

"I didn't give it to you forever."

"There's the closet."

"You're being difficult. You don't have the right attitude. Not about anything."

"Toward anything. You think I stole your jacket."

"Never mind what I think. I want it back."

"Take, take, Fein."

"Finn."

Slotsky smacked his forehead, then adjusted his glasses. "That's right. How could I forget? You're Finn."

"This is very disappointing. I expected more from you."

"I've got a lot of work to do, roomie."

Finn walked to the closet. "This one."

"*That* one?"

"Mine!"

"I wouldn't use it for toilet paper."

"Ha, ha."

"I used to wear it because I pitied you."

"Ha, ha."

Finn was out the door.

Millicent Coyle had brown hair, blue eyes, a slender body, and she made an impression of cleanliness and optimism. Finn talked most of the evening about Slotsky. He told her about his filthy habits, his obnoxious political beliefs, and, striking at the essential man, told her Slotsky was neurotically sensitive about being a Jew and yet never went to all-campus Yom Kippur services or any others held at the Concert and Dance Theater or the Hillel Center which had been designed by Miyoshi and cost several million dollars. Not once. He explained that Yom Kippur was an important holy day for Jewish people; at least that was Finn's understanding. They were parked in the lot outside the Kappa house. When Millicent didn't seem about to say anything in regard to Slotsky, he began to suspect she was waiting for a chance to scramble out of the car and just say good night. Suddenly she said, "I'll bet you think we're all alike at the Kappas'."

"Of course I don't think that. Everyone is different."

"I'll bet you do. I'll bet, for instance, you think we're all prudes."

Finn sighed. He would have found some answer to her accusation, but she didn't quite seem to be talking to him; to have sensed, that is, a particular subject in the air between them for the past several hours.

"Do you like to ski?" she asked.

"I've never skied, but I've thought about it. Up the mountain, down the mountain. Groovy."

She grinned. She knew he was making a joke. "Well it also gives you a chance to wear your après ski outfits, you know. You could learn in a minute. I know a guy who has a car like this."

"Pontiac? I rented it for the evening."

"I love Pontiacs. His is a Mercedes."

Almost impetuously, Finn said, "You know when I called you last week I was afraid . . ."

"My roommate took the message."

"Really?" It seemed relevant. Finn considered. Nothing relevant occurred to him. He plunged on. "I'd been thinking about calling you for a long time."

The confession made silence. He felt sweat blossom in his palms and armpits.

"For months I've wanted you to call," she whispered, leaving the silence intact. "Months."

Finn's heart pumped into the silence. His hand, like an independent caterpillar, pushed softly down the top of the seat and touched her cashmere. He looked at her eyes. Her eyes looked. He held his breath, bent toward her, and her eyes shut. Their lips touched. On her breast he felt murmur. They kissed, slowly drawing closer, pressing more and more of themselves against one another. Beneath

[174]

her skirt, along smooth tubes, he felt white, touched silky. "I wanted you to call months and months an' muns-ago." She crumbled in his ear. "Millicent," he whispered, shoving against her hand, her hard, fused tubes.

"Fein," she whispered.

"Finn," he said.

She pulled free. "I think I need a cigarette. I mean I really need a cigarette, but I'd like to talk a little."

Minutes later Finn was tapping the steering wheel with his fingernails. "I'm the only one who knows you're Jewish?"

"Well, actually, my mother converted years and years ago."

Finn drove to Slotsky's place and knocked until the door opened on Slotsky in underwear, his face deranged behind fingers shoving glasses against his eyes. "For Christ's sake. What the hell do you want?"

Finn shrugged, mumbled. Slotsky stared. The hall light made him look papery. Without a word Finn took off his jacket, then handed it to Slotsky. Slotsky frowned and shook his head.

"Take," said Finn.

"I don't want it."

"Take."

"No."

Shaking his head, Slotsky backed into the room. Finn shuffled after him, jacket stiff-armed at Slotsky's chest.

"Take it."

"I don't want it."

"Yes."

"Screw you. Get out of here, creep."

"Take it or I'll jam it down your throat."

"Screw you, Fein."

Finn lunged, stabbed the jacket against Slotsky's chest. Slotsky fell, smacking the floor with both palms, and Finn threw the jacket at his head. It caught over his head and chest like a lamp shade. Beneath it Slotsky screamed for help. Finn slammed the door. Slotsky shut up.

Alone and tired, Finn drove around town, the night droning, crowding into the car, pressing at the borders of his brain. He checked the dashboard again and again . . . twenty-five miles an hour . . . three-thirty . . . twenty-eight miles an hour . . . a quarter past four . . . less than half a tank of gas . . . ten past five . . .

And then Finn had a little waking dream in which he saw himself in Slotsky's glasses and Slotsky in his jacket, and Slotsky took his hand and he put

his arm around Slotsky and they danced in the head-
lights, big Finn, black Slotsky, like ballroom cham-
pions, gracefully mutual, dancing for the delectation
of millions until Finn hit the gas and crushed them
into rushing blacktop.

Going Places

Beckman, a day out of the hospital, barely strong enough to walk the streets for a job, carrying a ruined face that wouldn't heal for weeks and probably never look the same, was shocked to find himself hired at the first place he tried, as assistant to a paint contractor, and thought to tell his parents and write his girl to come back from Chicago and marry him, but, recalling disappointments with jobs in the past, decided to wait, not say anything and see how things went; to see if they continued to be real as the hard, substantial hand which had enveloped and strongly shaken his hand, less rough and hairy, but masculine, calloused by the wheel and stick of his trade, and a substantial hand, too; if not in muscle and bone, certainly in spirit, for in that shake Beckman was welcomed to the end of a successful interview and a life made wretched by rattling kidneys, the stench of gasoline, of cigarettes, of perfume and alcohol and vomit, the end of surly toughs, drunken women, whoring soldiers, vagrant blacks and whites, all the streaming, fearsome, pathetic riffraff refuse of the city's dark going places, though places in hell, while he, Beckman, driver of the cab, went merely everyplace, anyplace, until the sun returned the day and he stopped, parked, dropped his head against the seat and lay mindless, cramped, chilled in a damp sweater and mucky underwear, lay seized by the leather seat, debauched by the night's long, winding, resonant passage and the abuse of a thousand streets.

Everyplace Beckman, anyplace Beckman, he went noplace until two figures in misty, dismal twilight hailed his cab—a man with a pencil mustache; a woman with big, slick, black eyes, orange lipstick and Indian cheekbones—got in and beat him up while he begged, shrieking, "Take my money." They did and they left him for dead.

They left him for dead, Beckman, who revived in a hospital and asked for a newspaper with his first deliberate words, and read want-ads and thought about his life, so nearly his death, with a powerful, urgent thrust of mind entirely unlike the vague motions it had been given to while drifting through the dark streets of the city.

Something dreadful—running over a drunk, a collision with another car—might have happened sooner or later, but the beating, the beating, was precisely what he deserved, what he needed after years scouring the avenues like a dog, waiting for change to come into his life as if it might hail him from a corner like another fare. Indeed it had. Deserved, too, because he, Beckman, unlike the average *misérable*, could understand his own experience and, not without pride, he acknowledged the deity which had hailed him in the shape of twilight creatures and presented his face to their fists—as an omen, as a reminder of who he was—Beckman, son of good people who, when he pulled up before their two-story house in Riverdale on his monthly visit, became literally sick.

They were happy of course to see their son, but Beckman, winner of second place in an all-city essay contest celebrating fire prevention week, open to every child in New York, Beckman, the college graduate, history and economics major, risking life with strangers, ruining health in a filthy machine, it literally made them sick.

Laughing, telling stories, even a bit cocky, Beckman would finger the badge with his taxi number on it while his mother's eyes, with unblinking persistence, told him he was miserable, and his father, puffing a cigar against doctor's orders, sat quietly, politely killing himself, nodding, chuckling at the stories until Beckman left and he could stagger out of the room and grope down the wall to his bed. Behind the wheel, Beckman flicked the ignition key, squinted his mind's eye and saw his father prostrate with a headache, and Beckman gunned the motor, gunned house and street, his mother's eyes and father's rotten heart and headache.

There had been omens in his life not so damaging, if hair loss, shortness of breath, and wrinkles around the eyes and mouth were omens, but death had never been so close and tangible, and Beckman had never thought, "I am going to die," as he had, sprawled begging, writhing on the floor of his cab. Oh, he had felt the proximity of annihilation just passing a strange man on a dark street or making love to his girl, but the thrill of imminent nothing always came to nothing, gone before he might study it, leaving him merely angry or vacant and low. But now, like Pascal emerging from the carriage after nearly falling from it to his death, like Dostoevsky collapsed against the wall scribbling notes as the firing squad, dissolved by the witty czar, walked off giggling, like Lazarus rising, Beckman was revived, forever qualified and so profoundly reminded of himself he felt like someone else.

Hitting him, the woman cried, "Hey, hey, Beckman," a series of words chanted with the flat exuberance and dull inertia of a work song, repeated without change in pitch or intensity while fists rocked his skull and Beckman thrashed in the darkness, flapped his hands and begged them to take his money and continued begging as they dragged him by his hair over the front seat and onto the floor in back where the mat reeked of whiskey, stale butts, the corruption of lungs, and a million yards of bowel. "Hell your lousy money, Beckman," said the woman, her spikes in his face and ribs as the man, squealing with effort, pummeled straight down into Beckman's groin. But the punches and kicks were heralds, however brutal, bearing oracles of his genius, the bludgeoning shapers of himself if properly understood. Years ago he should have had this job with the paint contractor, a steady salary and his nights to sleep in.

He would write his girl this first day after work, thought Beckman, a letter of impressions, feelings, hopes, and the specific promise of their future, for now he wanted to get married, and his small, gray eyes saw themselves reading that line as he leaned toward the mirror and shaved around the welts and scabs. His brows showed the puffed ridges of a pug's

discolored, brutalized flesh where a billion capillaries
had been mashed and meat-hammered to the con-
sistency of stone. Ugly, but not meaningless, and
Beckman could even feel glad there had been nothing worse, no brain damage, no broken eardrum, no
blindness, and could indeed see qualities that pleased
him in the petrified, moiled meat, Hardness and
Danger, not in his face or in his soul before the beating, but there now as in the faces of junkies, whores,
bums, pimps, and bar fighters, the city's most deeply
kicked, stabbed, and slashed, whom he had carried
to and fro in his cab; memento moris twisted into
living flesh reflected in his rear-view mirror, reflected
now in his bathroom mirror, like the rock formations
of aboriginal desert and plateau where snakes, lizards, and eagles subsist and life is true and bleak,
where all things move in pure, deep knowledge of
right and wrong or else they die. Beckman whispered, "They die," and the ruined flesh gave sub-
stance to the cocky twist of his head, his manner of
speaking out of the side of his mouth and twisting
his head as though whomever he addressed lived on
his hip, though he himself was a few inches less than
average height. The sense of his small hands flapped
suddenly in his mind as the furies dragged him over
the seat like a dumb, insentient bag, though he
shrieked take his money, which they would take any-

way, and his body refused to yield its hideous residue
of consciousness even as they mercilessly refused to
grant it any. He couldn't remember when he had
passed out or ceased to feel pain or his voice had
stopped, but thought now that he had continued
screaming after he had stopped thinking or moving,
and that they had continued beating him until his
undeliberate, importunate voice stopped of its own.
They couldn't have been human and so persisted, but
had to have been sublime things which had seized
Beckman as the spirit seizes the prophet, twists his
bones and makes him bleed in agonies of knowledge.
Beckman, so gifted, saw himself like the Trojan Cas-
sandra, battered, raped on the rowing benches by
Agamemnon's men, and she was Apollo's thing. But
then he looked into the mirror, looked at the lumps
above his eyes and at the flesh burned green and blue
around his mouth. Not a shaman's face. He pulled
his tongue through space once filled by an eyetooth
and molar, licked sheer, delicate gum.

Enough, this was another Beckman. In truth,
no prophet, but neither a bag scrunched into leather,
glass, and steel, commanded by anyone to stop, go,
ache, count change out of nasty fingers, breathe gas
and hear youth ticked away in nickels. This was
Beckman among painters, learning the business, gallon can in each hand, surveying the great hollow

[187]

vault of the factory which he and the men were come
to paint. High brick walls seemed not to restrict but
merely to pose theoretical demarcations in all the
space now his. He and the gang of painters trudged
with cans, brushes, and ropes up a wall toward the
sky and the factory's clangor dropped beneath them
to a dull, general boom like a distant sea. The light
they rose toward grew sharper and whiter as they entered it climbing the narrow stairway that shivered
beneath their feet. Paint cans knocked the sides of
Beckman's legs, the loops cut thin channels into his
palms. At the top of the factory, against the white,
skylighted morning, they settled their equipment on
a steel platform. The men stirred cans of paint, attached ropes to the pipes that ran along beneath the
skylight, and moved out on swings into the volumi-
nous air. Beckman stood back on the platform trying
to look shrewdly into the nature of these things and
feel his relevance. The sun drifted toward the vertical and blazed through the skylight. It drilled the top
of his head as he concentrated on a painter swinging
ten feet out from the edge of the platform, his arm
and trunk like a heavy appendage dangling from his
hand. His feet jerked in vast nothing. His swing
was suspended from a pipe running beside the one
he painted, and as he moved farther from the platform he left yards of gleaming orange behind him.

Beckman felt his breathing quicken as he leaned
after the long smack and drag of the painter's brush.
Repeated, overlapped, and soon, between Beckman
and the painter, burned thirty feet of the hot, brilliant color. Beckman yearned to participate, confront
unpainted steel, paint it, see it become a fresh, different thing as he dissolved in the ritual of strokes. The
painter stopped working and looked at him. A vein
split the man's temple down the center and forked
like the root of a tree. Flecks of orange dazzled on his
cheeks. He pointed with his brush to a can near the
edge of the platform and Beckman snapped it up,
stepped to the edge and held it out into the air toward
the painter. Thus, delivering the can, he delivered
himself, grabbed life in the loop and hoisted it like a
gallon of his own blood, swinging it out like a mighty
bowler into the future. Concrete floor, towering
walls, steeping light hosannaed while Beckman's
arm stiffened and shuddered from wrist to mooring
tendons in his neck as he held the stance, leaned
with the heavy can like an allegorical statue: Man
Reaching. The painter grinned, shook his head, and
Beckman saw in a flash blinding blindness that his
effort to reach thirty feet was imbecilic. His head
wrenched back for the cocky vantage of height and
relieved his stance of allegory. He shuffled backward
with a self-mocking shrug and set down the can as if

lifting it in the first place had been a mistake. The painter's grin became a smile and he tapped the pipe to which his swing was attached. Beckman understood—deliver the can by crawling down the pipe. Aggravation ripped his heart. A sense of his life constituted of moments like this, inept and freakish, when spirit, muscle, and bone failed to levels less than thing, a black lump of time, flew out of his occipital cup like a flung clod and went streaming down the inside of his skull with the creepy feel of slapstick spills, twitches, flops, and farts of the mind. But the painter had resumed his good work and Beckman, relieved and gratified, was instantly himself again, immune to himself, and snapped up the can. At the edge of the platform he stooped, laid his free hand on the pipe, then straddled the pipe. He clutched the loop in his right hand, shoved off the platform, tipped forward and dragged with his knees, thighs, and elbows down toward the painter. His feet dangled, his eyes dug into the pipe, and he pushed. He dragged like a worm and didn't think or feel what he did. Fifteen feet from the edge of the platform he stopped to adjust his grip on the can, heavier now and swinging enough to make him feel uneasy about his right side and make him tighten his grip on the left so hard he pitched left. The can jerked up, both legs squeezed the pipe, and a tremor set into his calves and shanks, moving toward his buttocks and lower back.

Beckman squeezed the pipe with his legs and arms and slipped his left hand gradually under the pipe to cup its belly. His right hand, clutching the loop of the can, hung straight down, and Beckman leaned his chin against the pipe and listened to his shirt buttons rasp against steel. He breathed slowly to minimize the rasping and gaped down the pipe at the hard, curved flare of morning light. His knees felt through cloth to steel and the pipe's belly was slick in his palm. The tremor, in his shoulders now, moved up toward the muscles of his neck. Against his mouth he smelled, then tasted, steel as it turned rancid with sweat and spit. He felt water pour slowly, beyond his will, into his pants as it had when they hit him and hit him for no reason and he twisted and shrieked on the floor of his cab. He felt the impulse to move and did not want to look around into the vacuous air, nor to imagine the beating or the possibility that the tremor in his chin and lips would become a long, fine scream spinning out the thread of his life as he dropped toward the machines and the concrete floor. He felt the impulse to move and he could remember how motion felt gathering in his body to move his body, how it felt gathering, droning in the motor of his cab, to move him through the dark av-

---

enues of the city. He stared down the pipe, clung to it, and saw the painter stop working to look at him, looking at him with surprise, saying as if only with lips, slowly, again and again, "Hold on, Beckman." He clung to the pipe, squeezed life against his chest, and would neither let go nor drag toward the painter. He heard men shout from the platform, "Don't let go, Beckman." He did not let go. The tremor passed into muscle as rigid as the steel it squeezed.